Mended Hearts

Angelina Disano

Disano Dreams

Terre Haute, IN

Mended Hearts © 2021 Angelina Disano

E-book EAN-ISBN-13: 978-1-7377612-1-1

Paperback EAN-ISBN-13: 978-1-7377612-0-4

Cover design by Phil Velikan

Cover art © Miramiska/shutterstock

Packaged by Wish Publishing

Printed in the United States of America

10 9 8 7 6 5 4 3 2 1

"Do not be dismayed by the brokenness of the world. All things break. And all things can be mended. Not with time, as they say, but with intention. So go. Love intentionally, extravagantly, unconditionally. The broken world waits in darkness for the light that is you."

— L.R. Knost

Prologue: Ice

She wasn't exactly a long, cool woman in a black dress. At five-foot-two, there was very little about Katie Williams that anyone would describe as 'long.' However, in three-inch strappy black heels, she thought she could at least pass for a cool woman in a black dress.

The short, slinky number hugged her curves, accentuating her narrow waist and making the most of her modest chest. The dress came to mid-thigh, showing off her short but shapely legs. She had on a rhinestone necklace with matching dangly earrings, and not much else besides a little mascara, blush, and red lipstick. Katie rarely wore makeup; she reserved it for special occasions like holidays, weddings, and slaying dates at winter dances.

She inspected her reflection in the full-length mirror. Her chestnut brown hair now hung just past her shoulders in soft waves, and she couldn't help but be satisfied with the results from her curling iron. She turned it off and unplugged it, checked her makeup one last time, and then realizing that she had almost thirty minutes to spare, took to tidying up her tiny bedroom. The walls were boring apartment-white, but Katie had added a ton of color with a bright multicolored comforter, yellow pillow shams, and turquoise curtains. She made the bed and picked up some clothes off the floor, making a mental note to do laundry tomorrow. She put her makeup away into a pouch and placed it in a drawer of her antique vanity. Looking around, she felt the room was sufficiently clean, so she exited her bedroom to see if Grace was ready.

Katie entered the living room of the off-campus apartment they shared. Grace was seated on the hand-me-down brown sofa and had her heeled feet crossed and propped up on the second-hand coffee table as she scrolled through social media. She looked up when she sensed Katie's presence.

"Hot damn, girl! Look at you. You clean up real nice, you know?" she teased, making Katie laugh.

"Let me see you," Katie replied. Grace stood and twirled around give Katie a 360-degree view.

"Oh wow! Grace, you're stunning!" Grace O'Leary was five-foot-seven inches of red hair and attitude. Her wavy hair was long, to the middle of her back, and a deep auburn. It was the first thing you noticed about her, followed by her unusual honey-colored eyes. She was wearing a long, emerald green fitted dress with a slit going all the way up her left leg.

"You look like an old-time movie star," Katie added, feeling a little mousy with her five-foot-two frame (well, five-foot-five in these heels), brown hair, and regular old brown eyes. At least compared to Grace. On the other hand, who didn't look mousy next to Grace?

The two had been friends since their freshman year when they were randomly assigned to each other as roommates. They had immediately hit it off, despite being different in many aspects of their personalities. Katie was a little quiet and a bit shy but was always happy and pleasant. She usually had a smile on her face and seemed to light up the room with her warmth and sunny disposition.

Compared to Katie's steady temperament, Grace was fire and ice. She was passionate, strong-willed, and prone to mood swings. When she was happy, she was ecstatic. If you made her mad, watch out. She would not hold back and would tell you exactly what she thought. She didn't mince words and said exactly what she was feeling. You either loved Grace or were put off by her directness. There did not seem to be any middle ground, at least that Katie could see.

For the last two and half years, they were pretty much inseparable. They had shared a dorm room for their freshman and sophomore years but had moved to this off campus apartment last fall. Since Katie was a business administration major and Grace was a marketing major, they had classes in the same building and often commuted to and from campus together. On this day they were going to the Winter Carnival Dance on a double date - Katie with her boyfriend, Jason, and Grace with Isaiah, who she really didn't know that well but had asked because she knew he was fun at parties.

Katie and Jason had been dating for about six months since the beginning of the academic year. Jason was Katie's first real boyfriend. She hadn't dated much in high school. At the time, she thought the boys were all immature and idiotic. When she came to college, she found a few interesting guys and dated casually, but Jason was the first to capture and hold her interest. They shared tastes in music, movies and books. They were both serious students who kept their grades up and didn't party all that much. They just clicked. Katie thought being with Jason was comfortable; she trusted him and felt relaxed around him. He was her first love.

Grace didn't do boyfriends. Grace did hook-ups when they were convenient for her. She didn't sleep around or anything. It was more that when she occasionally found a guy she liked, she was never serious about him. They never held her interest, and she was always too much for them — too opinionated, too honest, too direct. The lack of serious relationships never bothered her though. Grace wasn't at college for the boys; she was here for herself.

Once Grace was done twirling and had shown off all angles of her gorgeous dress and voluptuous figure (another difference between her and Katie), they checked the time and realized they had twenty more minutes until their dates were supposed to pick them up.

"Let's take some pictures," Katie suggested, and Grace agreed. They spent several minutes hamming for the camera and posted a few on social media. When they felt they had sufficiently pouted, smiled and posed, they plopped onto the sofa side by side to wait.

Grace asked, "How did your finance exam go, by the way? You never told me."

"Oh, it was fine," said Katie nonchalantly.

"By 'fine' do you mean you got an A?"

Katie grinned sheepishly, "Yeah." Grace recognized that as Katie's 'I aced it but I'm too modest to tell you' smile.

"As usual, you brainiac. I'm glad you're not in my classes. You ruin the curve every time." Grace commented wryly.

It was true; Katie was incredibly smart. She always performed at the top of her classes and had been invited into several honor societies. If not for the one B+ she received freshman year, she would have a perfect 4.0 GPA, which still irritated her two years later. Once she finished school, she wanted to go to Harvard for her MBA and had dreams of being a big-time executive in a Fortune 500 company. However, she knew it wouldn't happen easily. She knew she had to work hard and not take anything for granted – not one assignment, not one exam, not one course. With this mindset came worries, maybe too intense, about her grades.

Grace was more laid back about her classes. She did well and had a decent enough GPA, but she didn't stress over exams and relied on her innate intelligence more than meticulous study skills. She took the grade she got and moved on — no worrying required. Her future career in marketing and promotions would require innovation and an understanding of people, not a perfect GPA, so her grades weren't a focus for her like they were for Katie. Again, another way they were so different from each other.

They were still smiling when there was a knock on their door. Katie looked down at her phone and realized it was still fifteen minutes until their dates were supposed to pick them up.

"Guess they couldn't wait," she said jokingly as she got up off the sofa and walked to the door. The words "You're early" died on her lips as she noticed it was not Jason and

Isaiah, but instead the dean of students, Dean Jacobson, and an older woman she had never seen before. *Okay, this is strange*, she thought.

"Uh, hi? Can I help you?"

"Hello, we're looking for Katherine Williams," the Dean replied.

"I'm Katherine," Katie answered, completely puzzled at the unexpected visit.

"Um, may we come in?" The dean gestured to the woman who had a decidedly uncomfortable look on her narrow, pinched face.

"Of course," Katie replied, now suddenly nervous. *What the hell is happening? Why is the dean here at my apartment on a Friday night? Whatever it is, it can't be good,* Katie thought as she tried to think of some, really any reason, for a visit from the college dean.

Finding none, she stepped back to let them enter and took in the woman's appearance. She was petite, her hair pulled back into a severe bun. She was wearing a tailored grey pantsuit and holding a burgundy briefcase. She wore nothing on her face except a pained expression. *Who was she?*

Katie closed the door behind them and turned apprehensively to face them. The Dean appeared to be shifting and searching for words. He was older, maybe 60, grey hair, distinguished in his dark suit. He also was wearing a somber frown on his face, causing Katie even more alarm. She chanced a glance at Grace who looked as baffled as

Katie felt. Grace attempted to excuse herself but was halted by Dean Jacobson who suggested she stay.

"Katherine, as you probably know, I am Dean Jacobson. This is Dr. Myers. Katherine, please sit down."

Katie obeyed numbly, her mind now racing, frantically trying to figure out why the dean and a doctor were here. It was all so strange. She suddenly felt an intense feeling of foreboding, as if her life would never be the same. A chill passed over her and the room suddenly felt extremely cool to her bare shoulders and neck. She looked up at the Dean, who was still standing, and the doctor. What kind of doctor? What the hell was going on? They both appeared grim, and she wasn't sure, but were they looking at her with pity?

She realized in some deep corner of her brain that she didn't really want to hear whatever it was he had to say. She glanced again at Grace, whose face clearly told that her thoughts had gone in the same direction. Katie's heart started thudding wildly. She realized now with crystal clarity that whatever they had come to say was not good. *Something is wrong, oh God, something is very, very wrong.* She felt the color drain from her face.

Dean Jacobson's heart was breaking. In all his sixteen years as the Dean of Students, he had never had to do anything as hard as this. He wanted to come out and tell her, but if he was honest with himself, he didn't know what to say, or rather how to tell her the news. He looked down at Katie's expectant face, and all he could see was the little girl she must have been. The little girl she would be, for only another moment, until her whole world was shattered.

It was suddenly too much for him and he stepped aside, choking a bit, and nodding to Dr. Myers.

The woman came to sit down next to Katie. When she grabbed both of Katie's hands with her own, Katie's fear spiked horribly. Her heart was now beating so fast, the pounding in her ears was all she could hear. She started to sweat. She couldn't breathe. She fixed her intense gaze on the doctor, silently willing her to tell her what was wrong and at the same time pleading with her not to.

It seemed to be minutes before the doctor spoke, but in fact was just a few short seconds. The doctor, to her credit, only hesitated slightly, chancing a look at the Dean as if to bolster her resolve. Finally deciding she could put it off no longer, she looked back at Katie.

"Katherine, I'm afraid we are here under the most troubling of circumstances. I... your... Katherine, there has been an accident," she finished lamely.

Katie couldn't seem to think. *Oh God. Please tell me this isn't happening! Oh God, oh God.* She felt as though her heart had suddenly been torn out. Instinctively she knew. She knew but she didn't want to know! *Oh God, please let this be a dream. Oh God, oh God.*

When she tried to speak, she realized her mouth had gone dry. She managed to croak out one word. "Who?"

Dr. Jameson took another deep breath and resolved that she could put it off no longer. "Your mother, Katherine. Your mother was in an accident. She lost control of the car on the icy roads." She paused only momentarily before adding the final blow.

"I'm sorry, Katherine, your mother is dead."

1

Tired

Two years later

Katie had a headache. She was rubbing her forehead and absently wondering if she had any painkillers in her purse when her co-worker peeked over the short wall dividing their stations.

"You okay, honey? What's wrong?"

Katie looked up at Maggie. "Just a headache. It's nothing."

"Want some Tylenol? Here, I've got some." Maggie's head disappeared below the partition for a moment, and Katie heard rustling and eventually, the sound of pills tumbling around in a plastic bottle. Then Maggie's head popped back up and she handed Katie two tablets. Katie looked up at the older woman from where she was seated. Maggie was around fifty with short dark hair that was starting to gray. Her face was round and brown with smooth skin, and her dark brown eyes were warm and knowing.

"Thanks, Maggie," said Katie, accepting the offering. "Don't know what I'd do without you," she added with a small smile, thinking of the multitude of things that Maggie had done for her and her younger brother, Tyler, since her mom passed away. Katie had applied to this job at the bank not long after the accident. She and Maggie had hit it off, and when she told her new co-worker about her mother, Maggie had immediately assumed the role of surrogate mom. She started checking in on both siblings to make sure they were eating and sleeping enough. When Katie had mentioned that their apartment held so many memories of Mom that it was painful, Maggie even helped them find a new place. Two years later and Maggie was still looking out for her. Grateful didn't begin to describe Katie's feelings toward her co-worker and friend.

"Almost quitting time," the older woman said. "Hang in there."

A short while later, it was thankfully five o'clock and they, along with the few other employees, made their way to the employee break area to gather their belongings. After grabbing their purses and jackets, Katie and Maggie walked together to their cars. They said goodbye and Katie climbed into her beat up white Chevy Chevette. It had definitely seen better days. There was a sizable dent on the rear quarter panel from a minor fender bender (not her fault). There were a few dings in the front bumper (okay fine, those were her fault). The doors sometimes stuck, the rubber on the windshield wipers was falling off, and the car sputtered and hesitated when it was hot. But it ran and she was in no position to be picky about her mode of transportation.

It took about fifteen minutes for her to drive from the bank downtown to her east side apartment. Portland was Maine's largest city and though not big by most standards, had its fair share of big city problems, including heavy traffic. The stop and go frustrated Katie who just wanted to be home after a long day. She swallowed the curses that bubbled to the tip of her tongue and prayed to the god of patience. If there wasn't a god of patience, there should be, she thought.

When she finally parked in front of the three-family apartment complex she called home, she was hungry and more than ready to put on some comfy clothes and relax. She grabbed her stuff from the car, not bothering to lock the door. No one was stupid enough to steal her car.

She walked up the half-dozen steps to the porch, noticing that the white paint on the bannisters was starting to peel. She keyed into the big wooden front door, which was as temperamental as a toddler. It often either stuck so that you could hardly get it open, or else it wouldn't close all the way. Today it was stuck, so Katie had to throw her weight against it to finally free it from the doorframe. She huffed a little and straightened herself before picking up her mail by the entrance.

She took a few steps down the hall to Mrs. Napoli's door and knocked. Mrs. Napoli was the landlady who lived in the first-floor apartment. The old woman answered with a smile. "Hi, Katie." Mrs. Napoli had to be at least eighty and was probably only four-foot-ten by Katie's estimation, but she was sharp for her age and very kind. She helped Katie out in the afternoons by looking after Tyler between the time he got home from school until Katie got home from work.

When Tyler recently turned twelve, he insisted he didn't need a babysitter anymore. After some negotiation, they agreed that Tyler could stay by himself in their third-floor apartment as long as he told Mrs. Napoli when he got home, came to her if there was any trouble and abided by certain rules Katie had stipulated.

"Hi, Mrs. Napoli. Wanted to let you know I'm home from work. Any trouble today?"

"No, everything's fine," replied the old Italian woman. "But you ... you don't look so well. Are you sick?"

Katie smiled slightly. If Maggie was Katie's surrogate mother, then Mrs. Napoli was her surrogate grandmother. "I'm fine. Just a little headache."

The old woman tsked. "Are you taking care of yourself, Katie? You should take some time for yourself. You know you can't take care of others if you are not well yourself."

"I know, Mrs. Napoli. Thanks for your concern. I'm just tired from work. I'll relax tonight, I promise."

Mrs. Napoli smiled, showing her missing teeth. "You better. Have a good night, dear."

"Thanks. You, too."

Katie made her way up the stairs. On the second-floor landing, she stole a glance at the door to Mrs. Stephens' apartment. The middle-aged woman had unexpectedly died last week from an aneurysm. They weren't close but had been friendly with each other and Katie felt sad that she passed. It was a cruel reminder of her mother's accident. Katie felt sympathy for the woman's family; she knew all too well the shock and grief they were experiencing at the sudden loss of their loved one.

She trudged up the final flight of stairs and paused in front of the door of the apartment she shared with Tyler.

She always felt the need to put on a happy face for her brother. They had both been through so much, she didn't want to add to his worries by letting him see her struggle. Katie always tried to be strong. She knew he thought he should be the strong one because he was a boy, but she was determined that he stay a child for as long as possible. Of course, with all they had been through, he was far from a typical 12-year-old. Still though, she vowed to do her best to protect him, and that included not letting him see how truly tired and depressed she had become.

And so, taking a deep breath, she unlocked the door and entered into their small living room. She found Tyler sitting on the floor with his legs stretched out under the coffee table and his back against the sofa. He had a textbook open and was writing something in a spiral notebook.

"Hey, kiddo. How was your day?" asked Katie as she dropped her purse and took off her shoes and jacket. She plopped down on the beige sofa and crossed her stocking feet on the coffee table.

"Fine," Tyler mumbled. *Twelve-year-olds were so talkative sometimes*, Katie thought.

"Anything special happen at school today?" she prodded.

"Nah. Well, I guess some kids got into a fight, but I missed it." He sounded disappointed.

"What homework is that?"

"Vocabulary." *One-word answers are lovely*, she thought to herself.

"Need any help?"

"No." Silence followed. *Oooooookaaaaay*, thought Katie, *that's my cue. Not getting anything out of him today.*

"I'm going to start making dinner. Spaghetti all right with you?"

"Sure." *One-word answers are fine. They're fine. I'm fine. He's fine. Everything's fine*, she thought to herself sarcastically as she left the small living room. She made her way through the "dining room" that held no dining furniture and into the kitchen at the back of the apartment to start dinner. The kitchen was tiny with hardly any counter space at all. The stove and sink took up almost one whole white wall and the refrigerator and a window took up most of the space on the second. In front of the third wall was a small oak table with two chairs, and the fourth wall was taken up by doors to the back bedroom, the bathroom, and the pantry. It was all very cozy, as Katie liked to say, which was just a nice way to say ridiculously cramped.

Katie put a pot of water on the stove to boil and got a box of spaghetti and a jar of sauce from the pantry. She poured the sauce into another small pan and put the burner on low. Then as she waited for the water to boil, she sat at the small kitchen table and scrolled through social media.

She wasn't sure why she always did this to herself. Her news feed was full of former classmates and friends living their best lives, going on trips, getting married and having babies. She hadn't really had any close friends in high school, Katie realized. She connected with a few of them on social media, but they weren't friends "in real life" as they say. So she didn't know why it bothered her that they were apparently happy and thriving. Katie knew that this was just their highlight reel and that they all had problems that they didn't share with the world, but it still made her incredibly sad to think about what her life would have been like right now if not for the accident.

She would have her mom to talk to when she was sad or struggling, and Tyler would too. She would have graduated college by now and would have been well on her way to earning her MBA. She might have even already snagged a job at a great company, making good money. She wouldn't be depressed, maybe. Perhaps she'd even have a boyfriend or husband. She couldn't help but think back to Jason Chandler who she had loved or at least thought she did.

He had called a few times after the accident, but Katie had never talked much and never actually confided in him. At the time, she was afraid of opening the floodgates because she feared the tears would flow forever. She was probably a little cold to him, and that's likely why he stopped calling. Losing him had hurt a little at first, but if she was honest, she knew she pushed him away. It was for the best, she came to realize. She didn't think she could have handled a relationship on top of everything that was happening during that time.

The water was now boiling so Katie stood up and closed the distance to the stove. She measured half the box of spaghetti and broke it before placing it in the pan. As she set the stove's timer, she mentally shook herself to stave off the melancholy thoughts. There was no use thinking about what would have, should have or could have been. So yet again, she pushed all those worries away and focused on today. She could do today. She could do the next thing.

That was how she had survived the last two years and that was how she was going to keep on surviving.

The remainder of the evening was a lot like most of their weeknights. They ate dinner at the small kitchen table and cleaned up the dishes. Tyler finished up his homework and then played video games, watched TV or read a book. At nine o'clock Katie sent him to bed, and as usual, he complained that he was the only kid in his grade who went to bed this early. He finally went to his tiny bedroom that was adjacent to the dining room. It held his bed and a dresser and hardly had room for anything else, but it was covered with posters of his favorite baseball and basketball teams.

Tyler refused to sleep right away, his own little rebellion. Instead, he stayed awake on purpose, looking at the posters on his wall and thinking through his day. Middle school was hard, he was realizing. All the kids were so judgmental and so many of them acted so cool and confident. In contrast, Tyler felt awkward and unsure. He had no self-confidence, and he was terribly shy. He tried to fly under the radar and not attract attention from anybody. He did his schoolwork and went to his classes. He was smart, though not as smart as his sister, but that was okay with him. He looked up to her so much and really appreciated all she did for him, but he never told her. He couldn't ever figure out the right words to say. Some nights, like tonight, he promised himself he would tell her. Sometime soon.

Tyler knew that Katie felt like she had to take their mother's place, to provide for him and raise him in their mother's absence. He also knew she was sad a lot but tried to hide it. *Everyone thinks kids don't know what's going on, but they do*, he thought to himself. He wanted to help her, to protect her as much as she protected him. But there was only so much a 12-year-old could do, he acknowledged with some frustration. When he got a little older, he'd get a job and help with the bills. It was the least he could do.

He wished she had gone back to college after their mom died because he knew she could get a good job if she graduated. He wasn't entirely sure why she didn't go back, but he thought it probably had to do with him. He just never had the courage to ask. One day soon, he'd get around to that too, he decided.

While Tyler was in his room, not sleeping as Katie well knew, she was free to relax. She curled up on the sofa with a hot cup of tea and a small blanket. Often, she would watch shows or read a book until she got sleepy. But sometimes, like tonight, she did neither. Instead. she was engrossed in her thoughts, and okay, if she was honest, indulging in some self-pity.

She was depressed. She knew she was. She never felt like doing anything and never really felt joy anymore. She still went to work, shopped for groceries, and took care of Tyler, but she didn't want to do anything at all. If she had her way, she would lie in bed all day feeling sorry for herself. But still she pressed on, doing what everyone expected her to do. It had been that way for so long, she realized, that she never even questioned it anymore.

She thought back again to the sorry set of circumstances that led her to right here, right now. Her mother had gotten pregnant young and had run away with Katie's father when her parents kicked her out. Katie didn't know her maternal grandparents at all. They lived out of state and had never even seen her or Tyler, to her knowledge anyway. She remembered her mom crying when she found out her father, Katie's grandfather, had died. But besides that, her mom had never talked about her parents. Some wounds were just too deep, she supposed.

Katie's dad had left her mom when Katie was young. She remembered her mom crying a lot then too. Mom said her dad had "gone away." She figured she had been too young when he left to miss him. She didn't even remember what he looked like. He was an image in photographs to her, nothing more.

Then came the "Jack years" when her mom married Tyler's dad. That's when Katie's depression started. Tyler's father had been younger than her mother by a few years, handsome and charismatic. Her mom had fallen in love, and they had Tyler. But Jack had started to drink heavily, and by the time Tyler was a year old, the abuse had started.

Katie had to mentally suppress the image of Jack shaking her brother's tiny body in a fit of rage. She had confronted him out of horror and protectiveness, started screaming at him, and that's the first time he hit her. She and her mother took several beatings before her mom got the courage to finally leave. That had been when Katie was fourteen and Tyler, three. Katie had never been so relieved as when they walked out of Jack's house.

She had thought, or maybe hoped, that being away from him would take away the depression and horrible thoughts that went through her head, but she had been wrong. The thoughts, the pain, continued right up through high school, college and to this day. After her mother's accident, the depression was suffocating. It took Katie a couple of weeks to be able to do anything besides sit in the apartment and cry. But at some point, she recognized that she was all Tyler had, and the realization flipped a switch in her. His father didn't want him — thank God — so she stepped up to be his guardian. She turned off the grief and turned on survival mode. She found a job, and then with Maggie's help, a new apartment for the two of them that had the double advantage of being cheaper and not reminding them of their mother.

She had withdrawn from school that semester and supposed she could have gone back when things settled down. She had a scholarship, so tuition was paid, and she probably could have gotten a job to support Tyler. But she couldn't bear the thought of returning to school. She rationalized that she didn't want to move Tyler away from his home and school after all he'd been through. But in truth, she didn't want to go back to the apartment where she'd gotten the news and to the life she'd had "before." It felt like that life was a distant memory or maybe a realistic dream. In some recess of her brain, she knew the depression was holding her back, preventing her from moving forward, from chasing her dreams, but as usual, she pushed the thought aside. She didn't like to think too deeply about things because thinking led to feeling.

Nowadays, Katie had what was called "high functioning depression," which basically meant she still went about her daily life despite her condition. To Katie, it just meant she was good at hiding her state of mind from others. Most of the time, she laughed and smiled and joked on the outside, while inside she had horrible thoughts of self-doubt and sometimes even bouts of self-loathing. No one would ever know because she had never told anyone. Not her mother, not Grace, not Maggie. This was Katie's horrid secret, a burden she had shouldered alone for more than ten years. Sure, they might have suspected she was down and maybe even that she was depressed, but Katie had learned to hide things so well, she doubted they ever knew the depth of her despair. She was such a good actress, she almost fooled herself sometimes.

She supposed she should go to therapy or talk to a doctor, but she never did. It seemed to be a weakness she didn't want to admit to anyone and besides, acknowledging that she had a problem would mean she couldn't ignore it anymore. Or maybe, just maybe, the depression prevented her from seeking help because some part of her thought she didn't deserve it. So she went along with her life, doing what she had to do, doing what was expected and trying not to think too deeply about anything.

Katie enjoyed her moments of solitude because when she was alone, she didn't have to pretend. She could cry if she wanted to and not worry about someone asking her what was wrong. Crying by herself was another result of the accident. When her mom was still here, she could cry on her mom's shoulder anytime. Her mom had always hugged her tightly, rubbed her back and whispered softly telling her everything would be all right. How desperately Katie longed for that touch, those words now.

She knew keeping everything to herself wasn't healthy, but she didn't feel comfortable talking to the people in her life. She certainly couldn't lean on Tyler, and she didn't feel comfortable unloading her worries on Maggie or Mrs. Napoli. There was Grace, and Grace always listened, always took Katie's calls, always said the right things. But Grace wasn't here in person to hug her and whisper reassurances. She was busy living her fabulous life as an advertising executive, and that life was not here in Portland. Besides, that was the problem with mental illness. When you're struggling, it's hard to do the things that are good for you. One big vicious cycle.

Katie swallowed with difficulty. She acknowledged the knot in her throat but didn't think the tears would come, not tonight. Sometimes she felt like this, as if the emotions were too much and she just got kind of numb. It wasn't a terribly bad state to be in compared to being a sobbing mess, she thought cynically.

Checking the time, she dragged herself to stand up and haphazardly folded the blanket and tossed it on the back of the sofa. She looked around the beige living room. In her current mood she was actively annoyed at the beigeness; Beige carpet, beige sofa, white curtains, brown side chair (just to change things up a bit). Black TV, brown wood table, beige lamp. Maybe if she got some bright new curtains or some colorful throw pillows, her mood would improve. She decided to look for something flashy the next time she was at the store. It couldn't hurt. She could even let Tyler pick them out, or at least help, she thought wryly, thinking of his taste in clothes.

On her way back to her bedroom she peeked into Tyler's room. He appeared to be sleeping soundly, so she closed the door again and continued to the definitely-not-modern bathroom. After she brushed her teeth and washed her face in the tiny sink, she studied her reflection remembering what Mrs. Napoli had said. She did look tired, she admitted. The bags under her eyes were more noticeable than she cared to admit, and she also looked a little pale. That wasn't good. But seeing there was nothing she could do about it, she shrugged it off and went to bed. Not like looking fabulous was high on her list of priorities.

In bed, she rested on her side and stared at the crack of light coming in from beside the window shade. She tried again to push away thoughts of what should have been, that life when she had choices. Choices, she thought grimly. No one ever considers how precious they are until they don't have them. Not too long ago, Katie had nothing but choices. She had had her whole life ahead of her and thought she could be anyone and do anything. And then came the accident, and choices regarding her life were now few and far between, or perhaps they only seemed that way.

In that moment, Katie realized with startling clarity that she wasn't sure she'd be here right now if not for her brother. In those darkest of days, in the depths of mourning, she knew that she could have chosen to end her life and maybe would have if she hadn't had Tyler to take care of. It was scary, but unfortunately true. The thought was sobering, to realize you valued your own life so little that you only lived it for someone else.

She rolled over and vowed to push away the morbid thoughts. It never did any good anyway. Her life wasn't what it once was, and maybe would never turn out the way she had hoped. That fact she had accepted a long time ago. But because of Tyler, she had to stay strong. She needed to be there for him, to do what he needed her to do, be who he needed her to be. She would give him the best life she was capable of, and though it wasn't much, she hoped and prayed it would be enough.

Someday, hopefully, they'd both find some sort of peace.

2

Dimple

His mother was dead.

Matt Stephens felt he had to repeat the words over and over in his head, so he'd finally, truly believe them. At this point it still seemed unreal or like it was happening to someone else. He knew it was true, but his brain just could not seem to accept it. They said she went quickly, that it was an aneurysm, and no one could have stopped it. One day he spoke to her on the phone and the next she was gone, just like that. He was glad there was no pain and suffering for her, but the suddenness was horrible for him. He'd had no time to prepare, no time to tell her he loved her. He hadn't said goodbye properly and the knowledge was eating at him. Guilt and grief made a nasty combination, he thought darkly.

He was now driving to her apartment on Portland's east side to clean it out. He fervently wished she had taken him up on his offer to move to Boston near him or with him (he had given her the choice) but being the stubborn woman she was, she wouldn't leave her home. Matt didn't really have an attachment to the apartment she had died in. They had moved there after his father passed away and he had spent his teen years there, but then he went off to college eight years ago and never looked back.

It was no secret he had wanted to get away from this city, this neighborhood, this life as soon as he was able. He spent his teen years obnoxiously declaring it at every opportunity. But his mother had felt an attachment to the city and neighborhood, and even the modest apartment, that he did not understand or share.

His early years were happy ones. His mother had been a stay-at-home mom and had given him love and affection and chocolate chip cookies. His dad had worked at B&M Baked Beans and had made a decent living as a shift supervisor. His childhood was happy and safe in their modest single-family home in the eastern part of the city, not far from here. He had a best friend, Danny, who lived down the street from him and was as close to him as a brother. He had never minded being an only child because of Danny, and he had never thought about how fortunate he was to have a family, a home, and a trusted friend.

That is, until his father passed away. He had only been thirteen at the time, a cocky middle-schooler who thought he and others around him were invincible. But then Dad got pancreatic cancer and within a few short months he was gone. Matt had known his father was dying but the blow was just as hard when it came. It was so like the grief he felt right now.

Because his mother hadn't worked and couldn't afford the mortgage on the home, they moved into this apartment building a few months after his dad died. At that time, Matt was mad at the world — everything and everyone. He hated the apartment because he couldn't play baseball in his backyard or basketball in his driveway anymore. He was mad at his dad for dying and his mom for not having enough money, even though he knew it was stupid to blame them for things obviously out of their control. He was a typical angry teen who blew off school assignments and went around on weekends making trouble alongside Danny. They drank beer and smoked weed and ran with the wrong crowd, and Matt didn't care because he hated life, probably even hated himself at that time.

The turning point in his life had come at age seventeen. Danny had been drinking and decided to take his dad's motorcycle for a spin. He had wrapped the bike around a tree going eighty miles per hour. Surprisingly, when Danny died Matt didn't feel as angry anymore. Instead, he felt numb. First his father, then the friend who was like a brother to him, gone forever. He still had his mom, who he loved dearly, but it still felt like 'everyone' left him. He didn't want to experience it again.

Besides diluting his rebellious anger, Danny's death had another important effect on Matt's life. Matt decided that he wasn't going to continue to waste his days drinking and smoking and making trouble. Instead, he was going to get out of this place — this apartment, this neighborhood, this city — and make something of himself. He was bright and could learn things quickly. When he started working hard at school, he earned good grades and ultimately was accepted to a good college. He had to take out some loans, but he didn't care because he was finally free of this place and all its memories of loss. He vowed he would have a better life than his parents and that his children would have a better life than he had.

His mother had helped put him through college by working two jobs and picking up extra money sewing. He appreciated everything she did and wanted badly to do the same for her when he was able, but no matter how many times he tried to convince her, she just did not want to leave her home. They were different in that respect. She couldn't bear to leave the city she grew up in, the city she raised her son in, the city in which she had met and loved and then lost her husband. So, she stayed where she was on the second floor in this less than fancy three-family home.

He often felt guilty living in Boston in relative luxury while she stayed here in this tiny, five-room apartment. When he visited, he always tried to change her mind, but his mother had been nothing if not stubborn and always refused. And now, he thought a knot forming in his throat, he would never have that argument with her again.

He turned onto her street and noticed there were no open spots in front of the building, so he parked his Porsche down the street and cursed at the inconvenience of on-street parking. He walked up to her building, taking in the familiar sites of the neighborhood. Two and three-story single and multi-family homes were packed so closely together you could look into your neighbor's living room from your own. Some were in good condition while others were run-down and unkempt. The big, old oak tree still stood in front of Mrs. Napoli's house, its roots pushing up to disrupt the sidewalk. The house itself was still the same gray color but now the paint seemed to be a bit more faded and peeling in places.

Matt paused in front of the house and took a deep breath. He was here to do something he dreaded, cleaning out her apartment. He was not sure he was ready to tackle the task or the memories that would come with it. Maybe he should not be doing this alone, he thought as he keyed into the big wooden entry door. His best friend Joe had offered to help but Matt declined. Then Joe suggested that he hire someone to come in and go through her belongings, but Matt maintained that this was something he had to do himself.

He made his way up the stairs to the tiny two-bedroom apartment on the second floor. He paused in front of the door that separated him from what remained of his mother's life. How many times had he run through this door with excitement or anger or happiness to share with her? How many times had she scolded him for slamming the door or getting mud on the carpet? How many times had they stood at this door and hugged goodbye when he left for college or went back to Boston after a visit? How many times had she stood here and said she loved him?

He straightened his shoulders and mentally scolded himself for getting too sentimental. *I have to get through. I have to suck it up.*

He was just about to unlock the deadbolt when he heard the outer door from the first-floor slam shut. A moment later, a petite brunette came up the stairs and paused on the landing to look at him intently.

"You must be Mrs. Stephens' son," she said quietly.

"Yes," he answered, taking in her appearance. She was young, he thought. She had dark brown hair pulled into a ponytail so he could see her face clearly. She was pretty and … delicate, he decided. She was wearing gray dress slacks with a fitted blue button-down shirt that accentuated her curves without showing hardly any skin. Why that was a turn on, he had no idea. She was looking at him with a strange expression that he took for sympathy.

He nodded, and agreed, "Yes."

"I'm so sorry about your mother," she said again in that quiet voice.

"Thank you" he said, not quite able to meet her eyes. He was still struggling with his grief and talking about his mother made him upset. He didn't want to lose it in front of a total stranger.

"If there's anything you need, I'd be happy to help. I'm Katie Williams. I live on the third floor." She stepped closer to him and held out her hand in greeting. He took it in his larger hand and shook it. When he looked into her eyes he was spellbound. She had huge chocolate brown eyes that seemed almost too large for her face. Doe eyes. They were striking.

"Matt Stephens. Nice to meet you," he replied.

As he studied her face a bit more, he realized that she had dark circles under her eyes. *Why does someone so young look so tired?* he wondered.

"I didn't know your mother well, but she was always very nice to me."

"Oh, well, that's mom," he replied. "Have you, um, lived here long?"

He thought he saw emotion flash in her eyes, but it came and went so quickly he couldn't quite identify if it was fear or sadness. She recovered immediately and the vulnerable look was replaced with an air of determination. She schooled her features into a polite smile.

"A couple of years," she responded with more force and volume than she had used before.

He nodded and thought to himself that she was a woman who was used to pretending. She clearly was playing a part, hiding behind a mask. Matt knew that feeling intimately. As a college student, he had played the part of one who was at home with the rich kids and the ideas of ski vacations, new cars, and an endless supply of pocket money. He had gotten good at that role and learned to act confident when he wasn't. Those skills now served him well in the business world. As a CEO of a successful company, he no longer needed to act, but it was a useful skill to be able to sense it in others. *What are you hiding, or hiding from, Katie Williams?*

"Well, I should probably get to work," Matt said lightly, and then added, "I'll be around for a few days going through my mother's place. Maybe I'll see you around." He had no idea why he said it. He had planned to stay at a nice hotel with an ocean view. Why did he just imply he would be staying at his mother's place?

"Yes, maybe," she replied softly. She turned and continued up the stairs to the third floor. Matt couldn't help but notice that her figure looked just as appealing from the back. He turned back to the door and decided that maybe staying here a few days might not be so bad. At least there was some nice scenery.

—◦—

Katie paused at the top of the stairs trying to get her rioting senses under control. What just happened back there? When she saw the man at Mrs. Stephens' door, she assumed it was her son, but she hadn't been expecting that he would be such a ... babe.

He had dark hair that looked almost black. He wore it just long enough for her to see it curled slightly at his forehead and the nape of his neck. He had a strong jaw, a straight nose, and the cutest dimple on his left cheek. But it was his eyes that got her. They were dark, midnight blue. Katie didn't think she had ever before seen eyes that color. They were mesmerizingly beautiful and unique. He also appeared to be in good shape physically, with broad shoulders and muscular arms that showed beneath his white polo shirt. The shirt was tucked into a pair of fitted jeans that allowed her to see that his thighs were muscled as well. *Wow,* she thought. *Hot stuff.*

When they shook hands, her stomach had flip-flopped, and the heat from his hand had her tingling still. She didn't know what was wrong with her. She had never reacted like that before when she met someone. Sure, he was good-looking, but why was she breathing hard? It was crazy. He was just a guy.

Besides, thought Katie as her heartbeat slowed, he wasn't going to be around for long, so nothing would come of it anyway. Too bad, she thought. A gorgeous, dimpled guy in tight blue jeans would be a nice addition to her pitifully dull life.

3

Regrets

For the next two days, Matt was occupied with his mother's affairs. He had taken care of most of the financial matters, including insurance, social security, and creditors. She didn't have a whole lot to worry about in that realm, he thought, somewhat bitterly. But it was still mentally taxing. Now it was time for the emotionally taxing part — cleaning out her apartment.

If Matt was completely honest with himself, he would admit he had been avoiding this task. While he could handle the financial and practical matters just fine, the thought of sorting through his mother's belongings struck a kind of fear in him that he couldn't quite understand. But he could put it off no longer, that is, if he was still going back to Boston at the end of the week.

He had already checked in with his office and stopped at U-Haul to get some boxes. He decided to stop at Dunkin' Donuts for a coffee and ended up with a half-dozen do-nuts too. Stress eating, he concluded and figured he was allowed given the circumstances.

As he paused at his mother's apartment door, he couldn't help but sneak a glance at the stairs to the third floor. He hadn't seen Katie in a couple of days but had been thinking about her more than he cared to admit. It wasn't just that he thought she was attractive. It was also that he was in-trigued by her. Why was she so tired? What was she hiding? Why did she need to pretend, to put on that act? Those were the things that had been bouncing around in his mind for two days.

He shook his head as if to clear his thoughts and with two trips, got his donuts, coffee, and boxes into the apart-ment. He sat down at the small kitchen table and downed half of a glazed donut in one bite. As he chewed, he con-templated the massive task in front of him and wondered again if he should have just hired someone to come and take it all away. He could have easily identified the things he wanted to keep and then left the rest to charity. It would have been quick and easy. And yes, less painful.

However, some indistinct force was driving him to com-plete this chore almost as a penance. He needed to be here to touch her things, to let himself experience the memo-ries, to say his final goodbye. He hadn't said goodbye prop-erly on the phone the day before she died. He hadn't said all the words he wanted to say now — how much he loved and appreciated her, how much he would miss her. And that was eating at him. So yes, he was dreading this task, but he would do it anyway. He felt he owed it to her.

And while he was here, what would it hurt to have dinner with a pretty woman? Share a drink and some laughs? No harm in that, right? A date, maybe two, sex on the third if he was lucky, then back to Boston at the end of the week. Back to his life and his company.

He and his best friend and business partner, Joe Mura, ran their own computer company. As computer science majors in college, they had developed an innovative software. Through a connection of their professor's, they had secured money for a start-up while still in school. They had graduated four years ago and started to put all of their time, effort and resources into the venture. The company began to do remarkably well and for the last couple of years, both Matt and Joe had been taking home substantial paychecks.

Matt gulped down some coffee and thought about how stupid he had been two years ago when he first became financially stable. He and his mom hadn't had a whole lot when he was a teen, so he foolishly thought that having money would mean things would be easier. But the whole ordeal with Jessica had shown him that with money came an entirely different set of problems than he was used to.

Jessica was his college sweetheart. His mother always kept her at a distance, despite her five-year long relationship with Matt. Mom must have known, must have sensed that Jessica wasn't the right one for him, Matt thought now, but Mom didn't like to pry so she had never said anything. Maybe it would have been better if she had.

He started dating Jessica in their third year of college. She was beautiful, with her honey blonde hair and green eyes. They had enjoyed the same things and got along well, and they both assumed they would get married after they graduated. But it hadn't turned out that way. They had ended it just about a year ago, Matt realized, stuffing the rest of his glazed donut in his mouth.

Everything started going south in his personal life when his professional life clicked into place. That was apparently because the universe has a way of laughing in your face if you get too cocky. The money ultimately changed Jessica. It was a gradual process, so at first Matt didn't realize it was happening.

It started with small things like spa visits and pricey clothes, and at the beginning, Matt was more than happy to provide these things to her, to treat her, to spoil her even. But soon she was spending a lot of money on jewelry and what Matt considered indulgent if not foolish purchases. She wanted to plan an extravagant wedding and got angry at Matt for vetoing some of her more outrageous ideas. He began to balk at setting a date, not really understanding why at the time. But now, Matt thought as he munched on a chocolate donut, he had subconsciously been avoiding the wedding altogether.

By the end, things had gotten really bad. When Matt curbed her spending, she pouted like a child. If he didn't let her buy that diamond bracelet or those fabulous shoes, she accused him of not loving her enough. It was ugly and manipulative behavior that chipped away at whatever love he had felt for her. At some point he recognized that he wasn't as happy as he should have been, and then he realized he wasn't happy at all.

A particularly nasty scene over a $2000 handbag was the final straw. They had fought, and in the midst of the screaming, he realized with absolute clarity that he didn't love her anymore. He broke it off right then, causing her to beg and plead with him to reconsider. But he was done, and her fake tears no longer affected him.

That was a year ago, and the thought of Jessica still made him feel a little ill. It wasn't that he missed her or had any regrets. It was because he was angry at himself for being so blind and stupid to allow himself to be used that way. It was a lesson he would never forget, he thought, as he finished off his coffee.

His relationship with Jessica had changed him. He now felt wary of women wanting to be with him for his money. He wondered grimly as he stared at the white floral wallpaper in his mother's kitchen if he would ever be able to trust a woman to love him for himself and not for the material things he could give her.

In the past year, he had deliberately avoided any sort of serious relationship. He was one of Boston's most eligible bachelors and had been photographed with several different women at various clubs and events. He kept things very casual with all of them, holding them at a distance. That, he thought as he munched on a jelly donut, was how he liked it. He took out women on his own terms and never let any of them believe he was in it for the long haul. Simple, easy, uncomplicated.

Sometimes, when he was feeling nostalgic or had too much to drink (or both), he felt a profound sadness that he might never have what his parents had together. They had loved each other dearly and were truly happy being together. They were grateful for what they had, even if it wasn't a lot. They had a home filled with love and laughter, and they supported each other always. His mother had been devastated when cancer took his father, and she had never been the same afterwards. She had never loved anyone else.

As he finished off his jelly donut, Matt admitted that he doubted any woman would ever feel that way about him, and a deep ache in his chest accompanied this realization. At times, he wondered if his newfound wealth would actually prevent him from having what his parents had together. He let out a harsh laugh. He had worked so hard for so long to have the financial stability his parents lacked, but ultimately, that wealth might prevent him from having the most valuable thing they possessed.

His thoughts turned to Katie. Who was she? What was she like? What was important to her? Could she be someone he could be with and not have the money get in the way? He had to stop his thoughts from going further down that path. Throwing his coffee cup into the trash can, he reminded himself that he was only here for a few more days and then he was going back to Boston for good. Thinking anything long-term about Katie was not realistic. Maybe a date or two or three, maybe some diversion for the duration of his visit. But nothing serious would come of it, nothing serious *could* come of it. His life was in Boston, and she was not.

He grabbed a couple of boxes and headed to the bedroom. Thinking about something he couldn't have was not productive, and right now, his focus had to be on this unpleasant task in front of him. He would do what he had to do, pay his penance, and try to escape with as little emotional turmoil as possible. Then he could get back to Boston and try to figure out how to live his life without his mother.

4

Daydreaming

Katie was daydreaming. About handsome men with black hair and midnight blue eyes. Okay, well, one particular handsome man, with a cute dimple and muscles and nice legs and… wait, what was she supposed to be doing?

Katie swore silently. She was trying to close out her drawer before her lunch break and lost count. Again. *Focus, Katie!* She admonished herself. Maggie peeked her head over the short wall separating their workspaces, noticing Katie was delayed.

"Everything okay over there?" she asked tentatively. She had noticed Katie was a little off today and sensed something was wrong.

"Yes," said Katie after finally managing to count accurately. "Ready for lunch?" Maggie agreed, and they made their way to the break room. They sat down and took out their lunches from home. Maggie asked, "So what's with you? You've been distracted all day."

Katie was nibbling on a carrot stick and staring out the window. She belatedly realized that Maggie had said something.

"Oh, sorry. What was that? I was distracted."

Maggie rolled her eyes with exasperation but said nothing. Clearly something was up with Katie but getting it out of her was another matter. Katie was a private person. Maggie sensed that she kept a whole lot bottled up inside. She wished Katie would confide in her, allow her to share the burdens, but thought Katie had some misguided need to do everything on her own.

So when Katie offered, unsolicited, "It's a guy," Maggie nearly choked on her broccoli. Katie hadn't, to Maggie's knowledge anyway, dated anyone in the two years she'd known her. She didn't seem all that interested in guys either, judging by the way she always blew off that cute lawyer who came in and flirted with her. So to hear her freely admit she was preoccupied thinking about a guy was surprising to Maggie, to say the least. She continued chewing her broccoli and used some water to wash it down, hoping Katie would open up some more. She got her wish.

Katie turned to meet Maggie's expectant eyes and smiled, shyly. "I met him two days ago. Remember I told you my neighbor died? Well, it's her son. I met him in the stairwell and found him… attractive." *Ha*, thought Katie. *That was a mild way of putting it. More like smoking hot, Greek god, take me to bed and…* Maggie had said something, but Katie hadn't been paying attention.

"Sorry, what?"

"Geez, Katie. I lost you there again. This must be some guy."

Katie smiled again, her eyes lighting up a little. "He was really very good looking. But more than that. He lost his mom suddenly. Like I did. And I guess I just sympathize with him, you know?"

Maggie only chewed on her chicken salad sandwich and raised an eyebrow. Katie looked down sheepishly. "Okay, fine. He was really cute too. And I haven't… dated anyone in a long time."

Now we're getting to the good stuff, thought Maggie. "So why don't you ask him out?"

Katie shook her head, "Nah. I've never seen him before. He probably doesn't live around here anyway. And besides, Tyler…"

"What about Tyler?"

"I just don't know how he'd react," Katie said, realizing that this sounded lame even to her own ears.

Maggie put down her sandwich and pinned Katie with a serious look. "You know, you're allowed to have a life, to do something for yourself. Not everything has to be about Tyler."

Katie looked away. She knew logically that Maggie was right, but she'd gotten so used to putting herself last, it seemed hard to chase something she wanted now. And she hadn't dated or… other stuff… in a long time, not since Jason. But the thought was appealing.

"Maybe," she allowed. "I'd want to see how Tyler would feel though."

"A few dates never hurt anyone, Katie. Why not have some fun for a change? Why not let loose a little?"

Wait, was Maggie telling her she needed to get laid? Katie frowned slightly. Not that she hadn't considered that option with Matt and his cute dimple and gorgeous eyes and…

"Katie? Hello? Wow. You've got it bad, girl," Maggie said, shaking her head. "I think you should go for it, but that's all I'm going to say. You don't need someone telling you what to do, I know."

Katie glanced briefly at her friend. *Maybe,* she thought to herself. *I'll think about asking him out.* Maybe it was time to do something for herself for a change.

⇥⇤

Katie managed to make it through the day with only two other obvious lapses. At one point she had gotten up to do something, only to take a few steps and forget what it was. She had stood there for several seconds trying to remember, and Maggie had noticed and chuckled to herself. The second was when she got up to use the restroom and practically ran into Brett, their coworker, because she wasn't paying attention to where she was going. Brett had looked at her curiously. Like Maggie, he was surprised at her uncharacteristic behavior but thankfully said nothing.

During the drive home, Katie was deep in thought considering Maggie's suggestion. If she was perfectly honest with herself, she was a little intimidated by Matt. He was good looking, well dressed and probably sophisticated. She was mousy and inexperienced, having only really dated Jason seriously.

In high school, she had thought most of the boys acted like idiots. Those who didn't had caused her to be wary, given her experience with Tyler's father. She knew men could be manipulative, controlling, even violent. She kept them at a distance, earning her the title of the Ice Princess, but it didn't bother her at all. She'd rather be safe than popular any day. Besides, she wanted to focus on school so she could get into a good college. That was her ticket out.

In college, she found the men to be a lot like high school boys except they drank more beer. They were mostly foolish and annoying. She met a few who were more serious, but she was still reserved, not opening up easily, slow to trust. She dated only a little before meeting Jason at the beginning of her third year.

Jason was different from the other guys. Katie had been drawn to him immediately. He was smart but not annoying about it. He was popular but not pompous. He was a serious student who was intent on getting into law school. Though she was wary at first, Jason had earned Katie's trust and ultimately her love. She had trusted him enough to be intimate with him and he was her first. Then came the accident and she had come home and, well, she hadn't been with anyone since.

So here she was, at 23, having had very little interaction with members of the opposite sex. She knew logically she could ask Matt out for coffee or something casual and that it shouldn't be a big deal, but she was still a little afraid. Of rejection, of looking foolish, of pursuing someone who may be out of her league, or who might already be in a relationship.

She pulled up to her building, parked and walked to the door, still lost in thought. She opened the large front door easily — no sticking today — and ran right into Matt. He steadied her with hands on her upper arms and said, "Whoa, sorry. Are you okay?"

Katie was embarrassed. She was so distracted thinking about Matt that she had literally walked into him. Plus, he was so close she could see the stubble on his chin, and man did that look hot. She briefly wondered how it would feel on her skin before realizing that her thoughts had strayed yet again. She blushed profusely and stuttered out an apology. "Yes, I'm fine. I'm so sorry. I wasn't paying attention."

"No worries. I was just headed out to grab a bite to eat. Care to join me?" *Oops*, thought Matt. *That just slipped out.*

Katie's eyes flashed an uncertain emotion that Matt thought looked like fear or panic. Although he had incited many emotions in women — some of them unpleasant but most decidedly not — he didn't think fear was one. Her eyes were wide, and he realized she looked like a frightened deer. "Um, Sorry. I can't."

With that, she practically ran up the stairs, leaving him to stare after her in confusion. *Okay, that was odd*, Matt thought frowning. He could take being turned down, but what caused her to look at him that way, almost as if she was scared? She was intriguing for sure. Why did she say she couldn't have dinner with him? What was she afraid of? Did she have a jealous boyfriend? A controlling father? *More questions, more riddles*, he thought.

Realizing he had been staring at an empty staircase, he reluctantly turned toward the door, relaxed the frown from his face, and went out to grab something to eat. Alone.

※

That night at dinner, Katie was pretty silent. She was still mulling over her encounter with Matt and her reaction, which to be honest, was embarrassing.

"Hey, Tyler?"

He looked up. "Yeah?"

"What would you think if I went on a date?"

His brown eyes, so much like her own, opened a little wider. Tyler had never known Katie to go dates and he was surprised to say the least. And unsure. He didn't want anything bad to happen to Katie. She was already sad enough and besides, she was the only family he had.

"Who would you go with?" he asked cautiously.

"Mrs. Stephens' son, Matt. I met him a couple of days ago. He's here… taking care of his mom's things."

Tyler looked thoughtful. Mrs. Stephens had been a nice lady, so her son was probably an okay guy, right? Would going on a date make Katie happy? He wanted her to be happy, but he also wasn't sure about this guy.

"Is he nice?" he asked, searching her face for clues. She smiled sheepishly.

"I think so."

He shrugged. He was still not sure about this whole thing. But if the guy was going to be nice to Katie and it made her smile, that would be a good thing, right?

"I guess I wouldn't care. As long as he's not a creep," he responded. Katie smiled again. She wasn't sure what she was worried about. Maybe she had been ignoring her own needs and wants too much. Maybe Maggie was right that she deserved to have a little fun once in a while. As long as Tyler was well-cared for, what would it hurt?

"Thanks, buddy," she said, and he smiled a little back. "Now, let's get these dishes cleaned up so you can finish your homework." He rolled his eyes but complied.

⋟⋞

That night, after Tyler went to his room, Katie plopped on the sofa with a cup of tea and scrolled mindlessly through social media. She wasn't really paying attention to what she saw though. She was too busy thinking about how she had practically run away from Matt when he asked her to dinner.

She had been embarrassed by bumping into him, embarrassed (fine, and maybe turned on) that his hands were on her arms, and she had panicked. She was worried that she had seemed rude to him, and she hated that feeling. As always, those things she should have said came flowing from her brain now that she was no longer in the situation. Damn it, why couldn't she think of these things in the moment?

Katie was also a little disappointed in her own behavior. She prided herself on being able to keep her emotions in check and she had definitely not acted that way with Matt. What was it about him that flustered her so much? Just because he was handsome and had a cute dimple? She should have more self-control, she chided herself.

Katie remembered again what Maggie said earlier today. Maybe she deserved to do something for herself. Tyler seemed all right with the idea and as long as he was looked after, her going on a date shouldn't be an issue. She could do something that hopefully would be fun. Certainly, she was entitled to one date in two years, she thought as she finished her tea. She came to a decision. She would go on a date. With Matt. The thought made her giddy with excitement. The feeling was unfamiliar and refreshing.

Getting up to get ready for bed, she began planning. Unlike other young twenty-somethings, she couldn't just take off on a whim. She had to plan for Tyler. He was almost old enough to stay by himself, but she still wasn't quite comfortable with that unless Mrs. Napoli was around. She would check on that tomorrow.

Should she ask Matt to dinner? And if she did, who would pay? She wasn't sure of the etiquette. She and Jason had always gone dutch since they were both poor college students. Hmm. She could ask him to coffee instead. A little less intimidating than dinner and cheaper in case she ended up paying.

Yes, that was what she would do. Tomorrow she would ask Matt out for coffee. She readied herself for bed, satisfied with her decision. She was taking back some control. And for the first time in a long time, she had made a choice.

5

Choice

Katie hesitated slightly before knocking on the door of the second-floor apartment. She finally got her courage up. She waited for a moment, but there was no answer. She was suddenly acutely disappointed and was just about to leave when she heard the click of the deadbolt and then was face to face with Matt.

He was shirtless. He had on jeans, slung low on his hips, but his feet were bare, and his hair was tousled. She knew she had woken him up. She stood, unmoving, unable to do anything but drink in the sight of his glorious, half-naked body. Her eyes raked over his toned abdominal muscles and broad shoulders before resting on his face. He was looking at her strangely, seemingly amused. Several beats passed. Finally, he said, "Did you want something, Katie?"

Her name was like a caress on his lips. Her mouth went dry. Suddenly, all she could think about was kissing him and running her hands through that curly black hair on his chest. Her apology was lost to the windfall of emotions and the rioting of her senses. She looked up into his face again, into those midnight blue eyes that had seemed to darken in the last minute and melted. She wanted him.

He must have sensed her thoughts because he grabbed her wrist and pulled her against his chest. As she looked up to meet his gaze, he ran one hand gently across her cheek and through her long, thick hair hanging freely down her back. He was looking at her with such intensity, such longing, that her breath caught in her throat. A tormented whisper escaped his lips: "Katie."

She closed her eyes as a delicious tingle shot down her spine. He grabbed her by the back of the neck, pulling her to him, and then he was kissing her. It was like no kiss she had ever experienced before. It was hot, frenzied, demanding. She pressed closer to him as her body succumbed to his ministrations. All she could feel was the urgency of his kiss, the power of his need, the heat of his body scorching her skin through her clothes. She was dying from the sweet agony of it. She ran her hands through the curly, crisp hair of his chest and then moved up to his shoulders and around to his back. She reveled in the contrast of the hardness of his muscles under the softness of his skin. She never wanted the kiss to end.

Suddenly, he pulled away from her. Frustrated, she whimpered softly as she felt the coolness of the air where the heat from his body had been. He quickly pulled her by the arm through the door of the apartment. He closed the door, never taking his eyes from her, pressed her back to it, and then kissed her again. His tongue was running over her lips and along her teeth and she couldn't concentrate on anything except its hungry rhythm. His hand moved slowly down her back and further down, then he pulled her to him, up against his hardness. She heard a groan and realized it had escaped from the back of her own throat. She wanted him to touch her everywhere, wanted to feel the heat of his bare skin against her own. She began kissing him and touching him more fervently, her whole body alive with burgeoning desire. Her skin prickled with every nip of his lips, every caress of his hands. She was dizzy and clinging to him, desperate now to hold on to the sensations that were wracking her body.

Despite the fact that she had nearly wrapped herself around him, Matt again broke from their intimate embrace. She felt confused and hurt and frustrated as she struggled to right herself on her own wobbly legs. Then she heard it, the smoke alarm. He motioned that he was going to check it, but she couldn't bear the thought of letting him go. She resisted as he turned from her, refusing to let the spell be broken, but he gave her a wry smile and stepped away. She grabbed at him, and his name escaped as a plea from her lips, but he was too far away now, and she began to feel anger. The smoke alarm was getting louder and louder and she then directed her anger at it. It was taking him away from her and she still wanted more. She wanted more. She wanted more!

Katie jerked awake with a start. It took her a moment to realize that she was in her own bed with her alarm going off. Groaning, she reluctantly reached over and turned it off. Flopping her head back on the pillow, she closed her eyes and breathed slowly and deeply. It was only a dream.

Only a dream, but she was still trembling with need, her body covered with a thin sheet of perspiration, an unfamiliar moisture at the juncture of her thighs.

Wow. She had never in her life had a dream so real! She could still feel his lips caressing hers and his hands touching her as if they really had been there just a moment before. She could still see his eyes smoldering with passion, still feel the strength of his embrace. She shuddered again. So real.

But, Katie reminded herself with regret, it was just a dream. Not one she was likely to forget in this lifetime to be sure, but a dream, nonetheless. And she had to get ready for work. She threw off the covers and felt the cool air assault her hot, damp skin. She shivered a bit and then stood up on unsteady legs. With another deep breath, she faced the day.

By the time she had finished her shower, Katie was less focused on the dream itself and was now worried about how she might react when she saw Matt in person. She intended to go down shortly to talk to him before she left for work. How could she face him with the memory of her dream still fresh in her mind? She was sure that she would blush from head to toe with embarrassment as soon as she laid eyes on him.

Granted, he wouldn't know *why* she was blushing. He would probably just think she was being shy, right? There was no way he could sense her dirty thoughts about him. So she would feel a bit awkward for a few minutes, she could handle that. Compared to everything she'd been through, that should be easy.

❧

Katie was standing, for what seemed like the second time, at the door of Matt's mother's apartment. She had finished her breakfast and sent Tyler off to school, all the while assuring herself that this would be a piece of cake.

Okay, she admitted, *I was wrong.*

She was nervous, suddenly realizing that her rehearsed dialogue had totally emptied from her mind. Her heart was pounding, her palms moist. A thousand "what-ifs" flashed through her mind. *What if I really do wake him up? What if he is half-dressed? What if he says no?*

Katie, stop it now. Just knock on the door and get it over with before he opens it up and finds you standing here like an idiot. Now THAT would be embarrassing.

Good point, she conceded to herself. That was that. Taking a deep breath, she knocked quietly on the door, desperately hoping that he would not be shirtless if and when he answered. She was sure it would be all over for her if he was. Thankfully, her prayers were answered, and when Matt opened the door, he was fully dressed.

When he first set eyes on her, Katie was chewing on her lower lip and looking at him with something that closely resembled trepidation in those lovely chocolate brown eyes of hers. But again, the emotion seemed to vanish quickly. Not knowing her intent, he began with a cautious, "Good morning."

Katie's mind was racing. He was standing so close she could smell his aftershave, or was it cologne? He was neatly dressed as he was yesterday – in well-fitting jeans and a navy-blue polo shirt. Unbidden, powerful images from her dream popped into her mind. His gentle touch, his caressing whispers, his kiss. She was sure she must be blushing. Did he notice?

Get a grip, Katie.

His expression was unreadable, which seemed to chip away at any confidence she had. Averting her eyes from his face, she cleared her throat a little and began. "Ah, Matt, I came to... apologize for last night. I'm sorry I ran off so quickly. I um... you caught me off guard with your invitation."

She chanced a look at him and thought that his expression had softened, and his eyes seemed to darken a shade. They were so beautiful she didn't trust herself to keep looking into them for fear her brain would turn to mush again. So she glanced down, groping for the right words for what she wanted to say next, when he answered "It's okay, Katie. No problem at all."

It was said with such gentleness that her eyes immediately snapped back to his face to look for signs of mockery or insincerity, but she only saw concern and something else she couldn't quite identify.

His dark eyes held hers for what seemed like an eternity. For a moment, she was mesmerized, lost in them as if she was swimming in the depths of the ocean. But then she heard a car door slam, and the spell was broken. She was suddenly acutely aware that she had been standing there gawking at him. A hot blush quickly stained her cheeks. She looked away, again hoping he hadn't noticed her discomfort and suddenly feeling desperate to put some distance between them before she lost her head. Why did she seem incapable of coherent thought whenever she was around this man?

She cleared her throat again. It was now or never.

"I also wanted to ask you something. I was wondering if you might want to maybe go for coffee or something later tonight." He smiled and she was again struck by the charm of his dimple.

"Katie, are you asking me on a date?" He was teasing her, she realized as a warm feeling, originating in her belly, began to permeate her whole body. She smiled back, shyly, and let out a little laugh.

"Yes, I guess I am. Are you saying yes?"

He laughed then. It was a wonderful sound, rich and full. She found herself feeling strangely disappointed when it stopped. He was still smiling when he graciously accepted her invitation.

6

Date

Work, Katie realized, was much more enjoyable when you didn't have to think about what you were doing. She was on autopilot all day, and it was five o'clock before she knew it. Maggie had said at lunchtime that Katie had oscillated between looking pensive and dreamy. That seemed about right. Although she was excited about tonight, she was also a little worried. It had been a long time since she had dated, and it was not lost on her that the last date she had readied for was the worst night of her life. However, she vowed not to chicken out. She had decided it was time to move on with her life, to begin a new phase – the one beyond her grief – and she somehow sensed that this was an important first step.

When she arrived home, she checked in with Mrs. Napoli and asked her if she could stay with Tyler tonight. Mrs. Napoli agreed, as she always did, but this time she did something out of the ordinary. Sensing some kind of new aura about Katie, Mrs. Napoli actually inquired what Katie's plans were. Katie blushed and dodged the question, somewhat, by asking Mrs. Napoli if she knew Edna's son.

"Of course. He hasn't been around as much these last few years, but I watched him grow up in this house. They moved here when Matt was about Tyler's age, if I recall correctly." Then Mrs. Napoli got suspicious. "Why do you ask?"

Katie replied, "I just wanted to know, you know, what kind of person he is."

Mrs. Napoli replied with a sparkle in her eye, "Because you are interested in him?"

"No. Yes. Well, I don't know? We're having coffee to-night." Katie answered, caught somewhere between embarrassment and joy.

Mrs. Napoli smiled wide, which she rarely did because she was self-conscious about her missing teeth. "He is a nice boy, Katie. Go on your date."

"Thanks, Mrs. Napoli," Katie said, squeezing the older woman's hand gently. "I don't know what I'd do without you."

Katie hurried up the stairs, seeing no sign of Matt on her way past. The evening seemed normal on the surface. She made cheeseburgers for dinner and checked that Tyler finished his homework. But Katie felt far from normal. She knew she had to tell Tyler she was going out tonight, and she wasn't sure how he'd react. She worried that he would be upset, that he would feel she was leaving him, that he would be somehow threatened by this change in her life.

So, with a serious look, she sat him down and told him she had to talk to him about something important. When she said she was going on a date later, he scoffed at her and said "Is that all? I thought you were going to have the 'sex talk' with me or something. Geez, Katie." Katie momentarily panicked, *Wait, what? Am I supposed to have the sex talk with him???* She decided to put off that thought until later. Much, MUCH later.

Katie fretted over what to wear, although that type of behavior was something she prided herself on avoiding. However, she didn't want to appear too dressy or too casual. Nice, but not like she was trying too hard. It was a fine line. She finally settled on dark jeans with a fitted turquoise v-neck top. She also contemplated her hair. She brushed it out but decided against wearing it down. She pulled it back into a loose knot. With one last look in the mirror, she was ready to go.

She made her way down to Matt's apartment and with one final steadying breath, knocked on his door. He answered the door with a smile already on his face. "Hi."

"Hi," she said back, with a smile and a slight blush.

"Come on in a second. Let me just grab my keys."

Katie stepped inside the living room and was not surprised to find that the floor plan of this apartment was just like hers, only the décor was very different. Edna must have been a very big fan of florals.

"How's the cleaning going?" Katie asked, noticing a couple of big boxes in the corner of the room.

"Okay, a bit slow." Matt turned off his laptop and picked up his keys from the side table by the door. He was dressed casually in jeans and a black, fitted t-shirt, yet Katie thought he looked amazing. The shirt hugged his muscles very nicely, Katie noticed with appreciation. She reluctantly dragged her eyes from his biceps when he asked, "Where are we heading?"

Focus, Katie. "There's a café down in the Old Port I thought you might like."

"Sounds great," Matt said as they stepped into the hallway and started down the stairs. When they reached the porch, Katie turned to him and asked, "Your car or mine?" When Matt hesitated slightly, Katie replied, "You probably don't know exactly where we're going, right?"

When he only nodded, she continued, "Then we can take my car... on one condition," she said mischievously, starting to make her way to her run-down Chevette.

Matt asked, "What would that be?"

"That you don't make fun of my car. It is not much to look at, but it runs. Most of the time."

He laughed and got into the beat-up car, moving the passenger seat back to accommodate his long legs. "So, you've had this car a while, I presume?"

"Same car I drove in high school," Katie answered as she pulled out of her parking space. "Has a hundred and eight thousand miles on it."

"No kidding," Matt replied. He didn't think he had to ask why she had not gotten a new car. Probably couldn't afford it. The fact that she drove this beater while he bopped around Boston in a Porsche made him squirm with guilt. He should have offered to drive, but when she gave him the option of driving herself, it had given him pause. He thought it would be nice to avoid all the conversation that surrounded his car, including what he did for work that earned him enough money to afford it. And he thought it might be nice to get to know a woman without his wealth putting up an obstacle before they had a chance to see if they clicked. At the time, it had been too tempting.

"So," he said after a moment. "How long have you lived in Portland?"

"Pretty much all my life except a couple of years I was at college. You?"

"Grew up here. Left for college in Boston and never came back, to live, that is. Felt like I had to get out, you know."

Katie knew exactly what he meant, only she was still trapped here with all her dreams wasting away, while he had actually gotten out and started living his. She had to force herself not to be bitter.

"Where did you go? To college?"

"Boston University. Computer science major. What about you?"

"Clark, upstate Maine. Majored in business."

"Did you say you only spent a couple of years there?"

"Yeah."

"Didn't graduate?"

"Nope."

"Why not?"

Matt sensed as soon as he asked that this was somehow not a question he should have asked. She looked at him briefly, and with a smile tried to make light of the pain she obviously felt. "Things change. Priorities change."

He only nodded and wondered again what her secrets were. Perhaps tonight he would get more clues to the puzzle.

They were entering Portland's Old Port district, and Matt looked around and took in the sights that he had not seen in several years. Nestled between downtown and the waterfront, the Old Port was filled with historical buildings, narrow cobblestone streets, trendy shops, and scores of upscale cafes and restaurants. The area was active at night because of the large number of bars and taverns. Parking was sparse, but Katie managed to find a spot only a couple of blocks from the café.

"I haven't been here in a long time. It's nice," Matt commented as they walked down a narrow street off the main drag.

"Yes," Katie agreed. "I love the atmosphere here."

"Do you come here a lot?"

"Only on hot dates," Katie teased as they entered the café. Matt smiled as he took in the scene. The cafe was small, maybe fifteen by thirty feet. The walls were dotted with an array of artwork from local artists, some for sale. The wooden tables were old, and some were littered with graffiti. The wooden chairs were mismatched. Classical music was playing over the speakers. The whole place was eclectic and, Matt decided, charming. He could see why she liked it here.

They approached the counter and ordered their coffees. Katie took out her money, but Matt refused to let her pay.

"You drove. I'll get the coffee."

She agreed and thanked him, and they sat at a small circular table near the back.

Matt began. "So, you grew up in Portland and went to Clark College. How about the rest of the story of your life?"

"Not much to tell," Katie answered. "I work at Maine Bank & Trust as a teller. I've been doing that for about two years."

"How do you like doing that?"

"It's okay. It pays the bills." *Barely*, Katie added to herself.

"Doesn't sound like your dream job."

"No, it's not." She looked a little sad, he observed.

"So, what is? Your dream job, I mean."

"I don't know, really." *Just not this*, thought Katie. She continued, "I used to think that I wanted to be a VP or something at a big company. But lately, I don't know if I want the long hours and stress, you know?"

Yes, I know, Matt thought to himself. *Too well.* "Is that why you left school?"

"No." She hesitated as she debated about how much to tell him. She decided on honesty. "I left school because my mother died."

He looked a little shocked and very contrite. "Katie, I'm so sorry. I didn't mean to pry."

"No, it's okay. It's been a couple of years. It's better now."

"Would you like to talk more about it? Or should I change the subject?" he asked with a half-smile.

"It's fine. It was a car accident. It was all so sudden, but of course, you know all about that." She looked at him with compassion. "How are you handling it?"

"I'm getting by. It's hard. Sometimes you forget for a minute, you know, and then when you remember it's like a burst of pain and you feel like you lose her all over again." He answered honestly, and it choked him up slightly.

"Yes, I know," Katie replied sadly, staring into her coffee cup. "For the longest time after my mother died, I couldn't think about it, about her, without feeling like I'd been punched in the gut. Like the wind had been knocked out of me. It's like, your whole life your mother is there, and you always expect her to be, and you don't know how to be a child without a mother."

Matt nodded, trying to keep his own emotions in check. He had experienced just such a feeling, and still felt raw from it.

Katie tried to lighten the mood. "Wow, we need to talk about something less depressing."

He laughed. "Yeah. Let's. So, what about the rest of your family?"

"My Dad left when I was young. I have one brother."

"Younger or older?" Matt asked.

Katie was just about to answer when she heard a shrill voice saying, "Katie? Katie Williams? Is that you?"

She turned and unfortunately, saw Ally Stanford bearing down on them. She was tall, maybe five-foot-eight with long, bleach blonde hair, and was dressed in a chic pantsuit with a bright, multicolored silk top and carried a Coach handbag. Katie mentally rolled her eyes, sure that the handbag cost more than she made in a week. Ally had been very popular in school and had not been someone Katie had hung around with or even liked. But here she was, pretending they were best friends. This was not going to be fun. Katie gave a small wave and waited for the onslaught.

"Katie, nice to see you," Ally replied, bending down to give her an air-kiss. "I can't believe this! I haven't seen you since graduation. You look great."

"Thanks. This is my friend, Matt Stephens. Matt, this is Ally Stanford. We went to high school together."

"Hello, Matt," Ally said, eyeing him with obvious appreciation. "And I go by Allison, now," she said to Katie. "You know, professionally. Here's my card," she added, pulling two out of her handbag and giving one to each of them. "I'm in real estate. Are you interested in a new house, Katie? It's a buyer's market right now."

"Ah, no, not right now, but I'll keep you in mind," Katie replied, holding back a snort.

"You do that. And Matt, are you from around here?"

"No, Boston," Matt replied with a smile that was too charming and flirty for Katie's tastes.

"Well, hon, if you're ever in the market for a summer home, please give me a call. I've got some great properties up by Sebago Lake, and some great condos down by the beach."

"I'll keep that in mind," Matt said as he tucked the card into his wallet. Katie was irked that he was not going to throw it away.

Turning back to Katie, Ally said "Well, what have you been doing with yourself, Katie?"

"Oh, not much."

"Not much! Come on, now. You were the smartest girl in our class! Surely you have an exciting job."

If Katie felt ashamed, she hid it well, Matt thought. "I'm at Maine Bank & Trust right now."

"Ooh, banking. Very nice. Are you in mortgages or investments?"

"No," Katie said, "Customer service."

"Oh. Isn't that nice," Ally said, though her face clearly showed she thought otherwise. "And what do you do Matt?" she asked sweetly.

"Computers," he answered curtly. She had annoyed him, a lot, by belittling Katie. He was determined to end this encounter, and quickly.

Ally had begun updating Katie on the successes of some other high school classmates that Katie really cared nothing about. Since she was too polite to cut Ally off, Matt decided to take matters into his own hands. He just interrupted Ally mid-sentence.

"Ally. Allison. I know you two must have a lot to catch up on, but I've been dying to get Katie to myself, and well," he added, grabbing Katie's hand in a warm embrace and smiling at her lovingly, "she's just agreed to this date, so you can see how I am anxious to get back to it. Maybe you two can arrange to get together some other time to reminisce."

Ally seemed taken aback at his rudeness and his apparent pursuit of Katie, who was always sort of a wallflower in high school. But coming up with no appropriate retort for that proclamation, she simply said, "Of course. I'm sorry. Please do call me, Katie. We'll do lunch." With another air kiss, she sauntered from the table, and after purchasing a coffee, left the café.

Katie waited until she was gone to draw her hand away and bury her face in both hands. "Ugh, that was awkward," she moaned.

"She was a bitch to you," Matt said, a bit too forcefully.

Katie's head snapped up. "Yes, well, that's Ally. I guess some things never change."

"Was it true? That you were the smartest girl in your class?"

"Yes, class valedictorian."

"Wow. I'm impressed."

Katie shrugged as if that accomplishment was nothing. *Another piece of the puzzle,* Matt thought, yet as he answered one question, still others arose. She was an enigma, and he felt compelled to know more.

"She was eyeing you like a piece of candy," Katie commented casually, looking at him to gauge his reaction.

"What's the matter? Jealous?" he teased with a smile. The thought of her being jealous over him was somehow very satisfying.

"Maybe," Katie added cryptically and then changed the subject. "I could use a refill, what about you?" she asked standing.

"I'll get it. You sit."

"Are you sure?"

"Yes, I'm sure." As he made his way to the counter, Katie admired his physique yet again. She had a nice view of his rear end in those well-fitting jeans. She didn't think she would ever tire of looking at him. And she had to admit that his speech to Ally, however contrived, actually made her heart flutter a little. It would be so nice to have someone say that and mean it. She sighed a little.

When he returned with their coffees, she asked about him. "So, tell me about yourself, Matt. We've been talking about me all night."

"Me, well, not much to tell, I guess. You knew my mother. My dad died of cancer when I was 13. I don't have any brothers or sisters."

"I'm sorry," Katie said softly. "Are you all alone now? I mean, do you have any other family?"

"Yeah, I have some family in New Hampshire. My grandparents are still alive, and I've got an aunt and a few cousins up there. I don't see them much," he added. "I ought to make a trip up some time," he said almost as much to himself as to her.

Katie nodded, "And what do you do for work?"

He told her the name of his company, which she had heard of, but when she asked exactly what he did there, he was evasive.

He paused slightly. "I'm in management." He knew it was misleading, but again he had the urge to leave the money aside, just for one night.

Katie knew he was evading her question but didn't pursue it. She decided to change the subject. They spent the next hour talking about lighter topics. Current events, what type of books they liked to read and the type of movies they enjoyed. They found they had similar tastes in music, and both were Beatles fans. They spent a good twenty minutes debating the relative merits of Revolver versus Sgt. Pepper. Before they knew it, it was eleven o'clock and Katie said she needed to get home.

They pulled up in front of the building fifteen minutes later as they were finishing their discussion of techno-pop classics of the eighties and the questionable fashion that they inspired. Katie was laughing and having a great time as they ascended the stairs.

Matt insisted on walking her to her apartment door. "I had a great time tonight Katie," he said sincerely.

"I did too," Katie replied, smiling at him. God, he was so gorgeous. He was close now and she could feel the electricity passing between them. Would he kiss her goodnight? The mere possibility had her heart hammering in her chest. He reached up to brush his thumb across her cheek. Tingles erupted all over as her body awakened to his touch. "Can I kiss you, Katie?"

"Yes." The word was little more than a whisper. She was dying with anticipation.

Matt hadn't meant to ravish her, but when their lips touched, softly at first, he lost control. He felt a jolt of electricity that put him on edge. Her lips were so soft, and she tasted so good. After a moment he lost himself and became hungry with wanting her. He deepened the kiss. She wrapped her arms around his neck, responded to his every move, every touch. Soon they were plastered against each other, and neither was cognizant of where they were.

He wanted her, Matt realized, with a force he had never felt before. He could feel the contours of her body, smell the sweetness of her skin, and it was too much. He had to get himself under control before he lost it completely and took her right here in the hallway. Slowly and with an aching regret, he pulled his lips from hers. Katie looked at him questioningly, her eyes still smoky with desire.

"I should go." His voice was not steady, she noticed.

"You're probably right," she grudgingly agreed with a dramatic sigh.

"Have dinner with me tomorrow." It was more of a command than a request.

A small smile played on Katie's lips. "Yes, okay," she replied. At that moment in time, she felt she would have agreed to do anything he had said, she felt so drugged with passion.

Still fighting the urge to continue where they had left off, he reluctantly broke the contact between them. For safety, he took a step back and out of reach.

"Around seven? You pick the restaurant."

"Okay, that sounds good," Katie said. He said goodnight with a smile and then started down the stairs.

"Goodnight," she replied, turning to unlock her door, still on unsteady legs. And thought to herself, *Oh wow. That kiss was definitely better than the dream!*

7

Meatball

Matt was tired and grumpy. He rolled out of bed, not at all refreshed, and jumped into the shower right away. He had not slept well. His thoughts and dreams were haunted by one beautiful brunette with an infectious laugh and incredibly kissable lips. Half the night he was pleasantly dreaming about what she would be like in bed. The other half was spent awake, wanting her, aching with need, and wondering why the hell these feelings were hitting him like a ton of bricks. He was damn near obsessed. Sure, he had lusted after women before, some with quite a bit of zeal. But when he wasn't with them, he didn't think about them constantly. When he wasn't with them it was like they didn't exist at all.

Not so with Katie. What was it about her? Was it that he didn't understand her? What was going on in that mind? One minute she seemed vulnerable and scared, and the next she was confident and self-reliant. What was she hiding? Why was she pretending? He had so many questions he was dying to answer.

Matt turned off the shower, feeling only marginally better. He vowed to put her out of his mind, otherwise he would get no work done. He needed to check in with the office, make an important call, and review some files Joe had emailed last night. Then he had to continue with the apartment. He was more than half done, he figured. He had gone through the dining room, saving his mother's china and flatware. Everything else was going to charity. From the living room, he had boxed up the family photo albums and portraits and had lost about half a day paging through the albums and indulging in the memories that had surfaced. He had enjoyed that time, remembering how happy his parents had been, even if it hurt a little.

The guest room was done except for the sheets on the bed that he had been sleeping in. He had also cleared out the bathroom except for a few towels and was just about done with the kitchen. He could easily finish that and his mother's bedroom in another day if he tried, but if he was honest with himself, he would admit that he had slowed his pace. He was not in a rush to get back to Boston any-more. He was not in a rush to leave Katie.

Damn, I've got it bad, he thought as he left to get some coffee and donuts. It was going to be a long day.

⇥⇤

Katie sat at her bank window and happily hummed a Beatles tune. She felt happier than she had felt in a long time. She had slept soundly and deeply, dreaming of Matt. That kiss was so incredible, she shivered a little each time she thought about it. He had definitely knocked her socks off. She had never been kissed like that before. Certainly, Jason had kissed her passionately, or so she had thought, but he never made her feel like her insides were about to explode and her legs turn to jelly.

She was so excited and happy about the prospect of her upcoming date with Matt that she had been chatting with and smiling at customers all day. This almost got her into trouble when the cute lawyer came in and mistook her new cheery disposition for flirting, and the only bad part of her day had been when she had to turn him down when he asked her out. But still, even that didn't put a dent in her spirits.

She left work in as good a mood as she had arrived in, drove home singing along with the radio, and arrived home to cook Tyler dinner. When she informed him she was going out again and that Mrs. Napoli would be coming to sit with him, he had looked at her thoughtfully.

"With that same guy?"

"Yes, Matt Stephens. Is that okay?" She thought maybe he was worried or upset. He paused a little before asking again.

"He's nice then?"

"Yes, Ty, he's really nice. But don't worry. It's not anything serious, okay? He'll be going back to Boston soon."

Tyler still looked a little skeptical and was feeling a bit worried about his sister. Sure, she said this guy was okay, but he still didn't want her to get hurt. On one hand, maybe this date would make her happy, but he really didn't want it to turn out that this guy would make her cry. She was already so sad all the time.

"Okay, I guess. Can I stay up till ten, then?"

Katie rolled her eyes. "Sure."

"Make sure Mrs. Napoli knows it's okay."

"I will," Katie promised.

Katie decided on black trousers with a coral scoop neck top. She also decided to go for broke and wear her hair down, which she almost never did. But today was a special occasion. She felt good, and she wanted to look her best. Her wavy, dark brown hair was long, past her shoulder blades. She brushed it out and tucked it behind her ears. She was ready.

She bounced down the stairs to the second floor, hoping Matt would be amenable to the restaurant she had chosen. She knocked and was greeted with a "Hey" and a smile from him.

"Hey, yourself."

With her hair freely flowing and resting around her shoulders and a good deal of bare skin that was visible due to the wide neckline of her top, Matt was again astounded at her beauty. All he could say was, "Your hair looks pretty down."

She might have blushed a little. "Thanks. Ready to go?"

Matt nodded and managed to pry his eyes away from her long enough to grab his keys and lock the door. He was dressed in beige khakis, a dark blue polo shirt and brown leather shoes.

"I have a great restaurant in mind. I hope you like Italian."

"Yeah, I love it," he responded as they made their way out of the building. He walked behind her to admire the view.

"Shall I drive again?" she asked.

"That might be best since I don't know where we're going."

She smiled at him and teased, "Are you sure you want to get into the car with me? I could abduct you, you know, and take you somewhere remote and do awful things to you."

He gave her a provocative look over the roof of the car. "Is that a promise?"

She laughed and got into the car, tuning the radio to NPR. They talked about her day at work and his progress on the apartment. When the national news came on the radio, Katie surprised Matt by engaging him in an intelligent discussion about the Fed's most recent interest rate hike. By the time they had reached the restaurant, they were in a not-so-serious discussion about who was the sleaziest politician in Washington.

The restaurant she had chosen was a small local Italian eatery called Sicilia, which was located near the shopping district at the north end of town. Years ago, the building had been, strangely enough, a Burger King, but the brightly colored booths and floors had been replaced by tasteful and stylish décor. The chairs and booths were upholstered with black leather, and the floors were beige and black tile. A wooden bar with a large, sleek mirror occupied the back of the room. The beige walls were littered with photos of people from the "old country" and personal effects of the owner, including an old, autographed picture of him with Telly Savalas in Las Vegas.

Sicilia was famous for their fried calamari, their antipasto salad, and their meatballs. They ordered some wine, and Katie insisted on having calamari as an appetizer, even though Matt was not thrilled at the idea once she explained that she liked to eat it with vinegar on it. While they were sipping their wine and discussing why exactly Matt disliked vinegar so much, Katie, who was facing the door, gasped and covered her mouth.

"What's wrong?"

"Nothing. That man that just walked in. He looks like George Michael!"

"What?"

"George Michael, you know, from Wham?"

He began to look behind him when she blurted out, "No, don't look!"

He turned back, exasperated, and amused. "This is the only date I've ever been on that I've talked about politics, vinegar and Wham before the main course."

"Well, I guess you're just lucky tonight," she responded with a giggle.

"Will I be?" he asked, suddenly serious. She blushed and looked away. He thought the effect was endearing but was afraid he had put her off. He was just about to apologize when she retorted playfully, "Certainly not. It's the vinegar thing. It's a deal breaker for me."

He laughed and took another drink of wine as his smiling eyes met hers. He could not remember the last time he had so much fun. Katie was witty and could discuss business, politics, and eighties pop-icons without so much as batting an eyelash. She made him laugh and she made him think. He realized he was crazy about the package.

Their dinners arrived shortly. Katie had ordered eggplant parmesan, her favorite. Matt had ordered linguine with a meatball. She purposely hadn't warned him what was coming and delighted on seeing his incredulous face when his meal arrived.

"What the hell?" he exclaimed as the server placed his linguine in front of him, complete with a one-pound meatball the size of a grapefruit. Katie giggled, and Matt looked at her accusingly.

"You could have mentioned something," he said somewhat petulantly. "I'll never eat this all."

"I'll help you," Katie said with a smile as she began digging into her eggplant, "when I've finished my meal."

Matt stopped cutting his meatball and scoffed, "You're going to eat all that, after downing most of the calamari, and then help me with this?"

"Sure, well, probably. We'll see if I feel like saving room for dessert."

"How can someone so small eat so much?"

"Do I? Eat a lot? I don't know. I just eat when I'm hungry and stop when I'm full," she said as she took another bite of eggplant.

"The women I usually date wouldn't be caught dead eating like that."

She stopped, fork in midair. "Why not?"

He shrugged. "I don't know. Watching their weight, I guess."

Katie practically snorted. "That sounds kind of stupid. And vain. Everyone's got to eat."

"Yes, they do," Matt agreed. Stupid and vain. That just about summed up Jessica and the other women he'd dated since ending it with her. Sitting there across from Katie, watching her happily enjoy their meal, he had to admit that she was much more fun and much more real than the type of woman he usually went for. He couldn't think of one good reason he would want to date someone like that again.

"So, what would an obviously intelligent man like yourself be doing with bubble-headed anorexics anyway?" Katie asked.

Matt paused. He was not quite sure why they had appealed to him. He began thinking out loud. "I guess it was just easy. No complications, you know."

"Had your share of complicated women?"

"One was enough."

"Ah, I see now. Broken-hearted rebound dating?"

He laughed at her expression. "Something like that."

"Who was she?" Katie asked.

Matt hesitated. Talking about Jessica was still difficult. "Her name was Jessica. We were college sweethearts. We were together for five years. It ended – badly – about a year ago."

"I'm sorry. Five years is a long time. You never married?"

"No, it never seemed right."

"So what happened?"

For a moment, Matt contemplated how to describe the collapse of their relationship. "She changed, a lot, and I didn't like what she had become."

Katie nodded. "That's too bad. I'm sorry."

"So," he said, changing the subject, "How about you? Please don't tell me I'm your 'broken-hearted rebound' guy!"

She laughed. "No, not at all! There was a guy at college, Jason. We got along famously. It was a good relationship."

"If it was that good, why aren't you still with him?"

Katie put down her fork and wiped her mouth with her napkin. The memory was far away and still a little bittersweet. "When I left college after my mom died, we had nothing in common anymore. We had nothing to talk about. I guess I was the one who changed, or my priorities did. I might have... shut him out, I guess. Maybe I broke his heart," she finished with a weak smile.

"I'm sure you did, Katie."

After a moment he asked, "So, why didn't you go back? To college?"

She hesitated. She wasn't really sure why. It was some amorphous combination of grief and depression and responsibility to her brother. Part of her wanted to open up to him about Tyler, about her responsibilities, about her depression and grief, but she wasn't quite ready to reveal that much of herself. She didn't want him to feel bad for her. She had seen that look of pity from too many people since her mom died, and she despised it. She knew she would hate to see Matt look at her that way.

Plus, Katie reasoned, he would be going back to Boston in a couple of days, and she would probably never see him again. There was no cause to lay her heart open for him to see when their relationship would not be progressing toward anything serious. That last thought, though it placated the part of her that studiously guarded her emotions, was practically devastating to the rest of her. She was really starting to like him, and she chastised herself for forgetting, even for a moment, that they had no future together.

"It's kind of hard to explain." He studied her face, trying to read her thoughts. *Guarding secrets*, he thought and let the matter drop.

The remainder of their dinner passed amicably. Katie did not, it turned out, have enough room to help Matt with his meatball, so he left two thirds of it on his plate. The ride home was relatively quiet. While Katie was thinking about the prospect of another kiss from Matt, he was thinking about the prospect of what might happen after that kiss. He felt drawn to her as if an invisible current of electricity flowed between them. Even now, sitting beside her in a car, he was fighting the desire to touch her. At dinner, she managed to bewitch him even more, if that was possible. He could honestly say he had never felt this way about a woman before, and it scared him. It also frustrated him. He wanted her, and he didn't think she was the type to jump into bed with a guy after two dates. He respected that, but hell, that didn't make it any easier on him. He had the feeling he was looking at another restless night.

Climbing the stairs to their apartments, Matt was following Katie. Swearing to himself, he struggled to tear his eyes away from her gently swaying hips and her long thick hair flowing freely down her back. He was dying to taste her again, to feel every inch of her, to run his hands through her luxurious hair.

Katie turned back after reaching the landing and said "Thanks so much for dinner, Matt. I really enjoyed it."

He arrived at the top step himself and responded with a smile, "The pleasure was all mine." He closed the distance between them and stood only inches from her so that she had to tilt her head back to look in his eyes. She drank in the sight of him, looking sexy and intense in the low lighting. She wanted so much for him to kiss her again.

"You're beautiful," he said softly as he dragged the back of his hand gently across her cheek, down her neck, and into her hair. Her eyes fluttered closed as she reveled in the gentleness of his touch and the softness of his voice. "I like your hair down."

"Mmmm," was all she could manage.

He kissed her then, but it was not what she had expected. The touch of his lips was soft and tender. He did not rush. He was determined to go slow, to savor her taste. She yielded to his pace, to his mood, and relished every nip, every touch of his tongue. She felt she was dying a sweet tortuous death. She loved that his touch was so tender and gentle. She loved that he was caressing her neck and her shoulders with his fingertips and affectionately playing with her hair. Though the kiss was nothing like their first, it was arousing. She felt on edge, that the passion was bubbling just beneath the surface.

Matt too, was aroused. He had tried to stay in control and avoid a repeat of last night when he nearly accosted her in the hallway. But he had gotten in over his head because he was losing himself in this kiss, in the smoothness of her skin, in the silky texture of her hair. He thought with a jolt of alarm that he wanted her more now than ever, and for one fleeting second thought that maybe he was falling for her. He had to regain composure, to let her make her own decision, so with colossal effort, his lips left hers, though his hand lingered at her neck.

Her eyes fluttered halfway open, and she looked dreamily to him. "You are an amazing kisser."

She had no doubt that the emotion that flashed in his deep blue eyes was desire. "I could be amazing at other things too."

A heartbeat passed, then another. Katie warred with herself. She knew what he was intimating as well as she knew that he was putting the ball in her court. He would not ask, he would not push. It was her decision, her call.

"I'm not ready," was all she said.

He nodded understandingly. "Will you let me take you out again tomorrow?"

"Yes."

"Great. Sleep well," he said, placing a short, soft kiss on her lips. She stood there for a moment, watching him disappear from sight, feeling a strange combination of satisfaction and restlessness. She didn't know how long she could go on denying herself. She had foolishly thought that she desired Jason, that she was attracted to him. What she had felt for Jason did not even approach the intensity of desire that she had for Matt. She was going to acquiesce soon, she knew, when the time was right. Even if he left and went back to Boston, she was going to give herself to him. Even if she had only one night with him, it would be worth it.

8

Beach

The next day was a hot and humid Friday. It was May and the weather was unseasonably warm for Maine. Katie sweated through her workday, eager to see Matt that evening. When she got home after work, she wanted to have a talk with Tyler. If she was honest with herself, she was sweating about that too.

She wasn't sure how he'd react. He seemed to accept her going out with Matt last night, but tonight would make three nights in a row, and Katie was afraid Tyler would think this was going to become a habit. She wanted him to understand that this wasn't anything serious and that it was something that would help her feel more like a normal 23-year-old. She hoped he'd understand.

Katie found the living room empty when she arrived home from work and figured the closed door to Tyler's bedroom meant he was hidden away in there.

She knocked on the door. "Hey, Ty. Can we talk?"

"Sure. Come in," he responded. When she entered the tiny room, he was on his bed reading a book.

"How was school?"

"Fine," he answered.

"Any homework this weekend?"

"Nope."

One word answers again. Lovely. "So I told you this morning I was going out tonight again. Are you sure that's okay with you?"

"Yeah."

"It doesn't make you feel, I don't know, neglected or something?"

He peeked over his book to study her. Brown eyes met brown eyes as she tried to read his thoughts, to gauge his true feelings. She wanted him to understand that he was the most important person in her life, but that she wanted to do something for herself. That sometimes she wanted to feel like the young, single woman that she was.

Tyler was worried about Katie a little, but she seemed happy about going on dates with this guy and that was good. He wanted her to be happy. But it seemed like she really liked him. Maybe when he left, she would be upset and that wouldn't be good. Should he say something?

"You said he was going back to Boston, right?"

"Yes."

"So you won't be going on more dates when he leaves, right?"

The true words made Katie frown. "Yes."

Tyler put the book down to study his sister. He hadn't missed her reaction to his statement. She really did like this guy.

"Are you going to be upset when he leaves?"

She looked at him thoughtfully. He was perceptive for a 12-year-old, or maybe she was just too easy to read.

"I don't know. Maybe. But I like him, and I like spending time with him. You know that it doesn't mean he's more important than you, right? You're the most important person to me." She reassured him with a smile.

She looked pretty when she smiled, he decided. He smiled back a little half-smile.

"I know."

"So you won't feel bad if I go out again tonight?"

"No, I won't." He wanted to say more, to tell her how much he loved her and appreciated her, but again he couldn't find the right words. One day, when he was older, he would let her know. She smiled again and ruffled his hair, which made Tyler roll his eyes.

"Thanks, Ty. For understanding." He looked at her briefly and the words almost came out — I love you, Katie and I want you to be happy — but they didn't. Saying things like that, mushy things, was just too hard. So he just nodded and picked up his book again. She closed the door behind her when she left his room and went to get ready for her date.

⟶⟵

Katie and Matt decided to go to Old Orchard Beach, which was about a twenty-minute drive in her beat-up Chevette. Old Orchard was a tourist destination, mostly for Canadians and other New Englanders. The main street was perpendicular to the beach and housed dozens of small shops selling souvenirs, bathing suits, and food. The road parallel to the beach on one side sported dozens of condos, motels, rented homes and cottages, along with a few restaurants and shops. On the other side of the main drag stood Palace Playland, a small amusement park complete with rides, a carousel, arcades and game booths. Behind the playland and across the street stood an enormous miniature golf facility. At the end of the main drag, beyond a small traffic circle stood "The Pier," which extended a few hundred feet into the ocean, and housed bars, food stands, and shops.

Matt had smiled when she proposed their destination. He hadn't been there since he was a teen and had fond memories of outings there with Danny. Matt and Katie had a blast and acted like teens themselves. They had talked about nothing in particular but had not lacked for conversation. They had gone on a few rides, including the carousel. Katie had teased Matt when she beat him at mini-golf, and he teased her when he beat her at skee-ball.

At one point, Katie said, "Hey, Matt, before we eat, can we go on the roller coaster?"

"Sure," answered Matt, even though he wasn't crazy about roller coasters. He didn't want to disappoint his date. So they waited in line for the largest roller coaster in the park. Katie screamed through the entire ride. When they got off, Matt said "I can't tell if you liked that or not."

Katie replied, a bit shyly, "Well, I wouldn't say I liked it. I just ... Can I tell you something that might sound weird?"

Matt turned to face her, "Of course."

Katie continued, "Sometimes, since my mom died, I feel kind of empty inside and I do things just because I want to feel SOMETHING. Even if it's not completely good. Does that make sense?"

Matt thought a bit and nodded, "Yes, I think so." Katie was relieved that Matt appeared to understand, and the thought made her like this guy just a little more.

After that, they ate ice cream sundaes, and he kissed the whipped cream off her lips. They ate pier fries but didn't share since he was disgusted when she drowned hers in vinegar, laughing mischievously the whole time. They walked on the pier and joked about the cheesy merchandise.

Lastly, they strolled, hand in hand, on the beach after the sun went down. He was telling her a funny story about himself and Joe during their sophomore year of college. With each new twist, she was laughing and gasping, and finally bent over in a fit of laughter. When the spasms had finally subsided and she was able to stand, she found Matt looking at her with a foolish grin on his face.

"I really like being with you, Matt. You make me forget all my troubles."

His grin faded and he was suddenly eyeing her intently. "What troubles, Katie?"

She shrugged and turned away slightly, determined to not ruin the cheerful mood she was in. She tried to continue walking, but he grabbed her gently on the arm and she faced him again. "What are you hiding from me, Katie?"

"It's nothing. It's just... you're leaving soon, to go back to Boston."

"Yes, I am."

"When?" she asked.

"Probably Sunday."

"Oh," was all she said, looking down at her sandaled feet.

"Is that what this is? That you are afraid to get too involved?"

"Yes. No, not exactly. I don't know. It's just ... complicated."

He waited silently as she looked out at the water. Katie was thinking that Tyler had a birthday party tomorrow evening. He would be leaving around five o'clock and had planned to stay overnight at the friend's house. "Tomorrow," she said, making the decision. "How about tomorrow I make you dinner and we can drink wine and just talk. I'll try to explain."

Matt nodded and seemed satisfied. He grabbed her hand and they walked while he tried to think of a way to make her laugh again.

"So, can you cook?"

"What?"

"Can you cook? You said you'd make me dinner. So will this be a treat for me, or a punishment?"

She laughed. "Because you beat me at skee-ball, I'm going to dodge that question and leave you wondering."

"You're a pretty sore loser, you know."

As a response, she stuck her tongue out at him and bounded away from him. He grinned like a schoolboy. Hell, he felt like a schoolboy. When was the last time a woman stuck her tongue out at him?

He chased her for a short distance and caught up with her easily. She was laughing and her hair had escaped its knot and she looked breathtakingly lovely in the moonlight. God, he was falling for her.

"Your laughter is captivating, Katie."

"It is, huh?" she answered lightly.

"Yes. And your smile is stunning." She briefly averted her eyes from his face and was thankful that it was too dark for him to see her blush. He continued, "And very kissable."

When her eyes returned to his face, he kissed her, briefly, but deeply. It was enough to have her heart pounding in her chest. He motioned for them to turn back and again took her hand.

"You look pretty good when you smile too. I'm a sucker for dimples you know," she said teasingly.

"Yeah?"

"Yeah."

"What else are you a sucker for? That information might come in handy in the future."

"Let's see. A handsome face..."

"I've got that," he teased.

She tsked him and continued, "is not important to me." She finished while enjoying his affronted glare.

Katie continued, "I like a good sense of humor."

"Check."

"Kindness and compassion."

"All the time."

"Someone who is a good kisser," she continued mischievously.

"We've already established that."

"And the most important quality is... modesty," she finished triumphantly.

He laughed, rich and full. "Okay, you got me."

⁕

The man watched them closely, making sure to stay far enough behind that he would not be seen and recognized. Once he got a good look, he was sure. That was Katie. All grown up now, yes, but she hadn't changed all that much in the last nine years. And the man with her, he was sure now who that was. It was THE Matt Stephens, the CEO of that new startup everyone had been talking about a couple of years ago. The two of them looked mighty friendly with each other. How did a mousy little bitch like Katie land a rich and famous guy like Matt Stephens? It was almost unthinkable to him based on what he remembered about her. But regardless of how she'd done it — she was probably good in the sack — he was starting to get an idea that might just be the big break he was looking for.

⁕

The ride home was equally lighthearted and fun for Katie and Matt. They were both comfortable with each other and were having a splendid time teasing and laughing.

When they arrived back at the apartment, the mood was a bit more subdued. Their time was over, and neither particularly wanted to part at that point.

"Tomorrow, right?" Matt asked as she approached her door.

"Yes, definitely."

He moved toward her, and her heart skipped a beat.

"Are you going to kiss me goodnight?" she asked coyly.

"Do you want me to?"

"Yes. I might even kiss you back."

He took his time getting to her. They were standing close so that their bodies touched lightly, yet he didn't make a move, only stared into her eyes. She began to get restless as she waited some more, and her pulse began to quicken as she felt the heat from his body. Impatient now and tired of waiting, she grabbed at his shirt, pulled him toward her, and initiated the kiss.

He was in heaven. He was turned on by the force with which she grabbed him. He let her lead, let her set the pace, and it was exquisite. His arms moved around to her back and waist, and he pulled her against him. She moaned softly and kissed him more fervently. His mouth broke free of hers as he planted kisses on her chin, near her ear, and down her neck to her collarbone. She moaned again and he felt himself growing hard with desire. He worked back to her mouth and was desperately devouring her. She was kissing him back with abandon as her hands moved over his chest and up around his shoulders. They were both breathing hard as he managed a tortured whisper in her ear. "Katie, you're killing me here. Please, let me come in. Let me make love to you."

She shivered with excitement or maybe fear, and her body had almost convinced her brain to say yes, but reason slowly emerged through the fog of her passion. "I'm sorry, I can't," she said as she felt an intense pang of regret realizing that Tyler was in their apartment right now. "Not tonight."

"I have protection," he offered, thinking that was her concern.

"No, it's not that. It's just, not tonight, Matt, okay?"

He closed his eyes and tried to regain control of his raging hunger for her. Could he wait one more day? Could he survive? Damn it, he would have to. He planted one more soft kiss on her neck and a quick hard one on her lips and stepped away.

"Tomorrow then?"

She nodded and he left. Neither one slept very well that night.

◆◆◆

It was just after five o'clock Saturday. Katie had spent the day much as she always did – grocery shopping, picking up the house, and spending time with her brother. She was dressed in simple jeans and a pink t-shirt with no shoes as she busied herself with dinner preparations. She was cutting up vegetables for her baked chicken dish that she was serving with rice and salad. It wasn't fancy, but it was the only meal she could cook reliably that didn't involve something directly out of a jar.

Although she had not had a restful night, she was energized and excited for Matt's arrival. She had decided to tell him everything about her current situation, about her brother, about Jason and the night her mother died, about her limited experience. She felt strongly he needed to know and to understand why she had been thus far hesitant to jump into bed with him. And if he did understand, and he still wanted her, she was ready.

She put the pan in the oven, set the timer, and had just finished washing and drying her hands. Looking at the clock, she figured she had about thirty minutes until he arrived, and about one hour until she would serve dinner. Everything was on schedule.

She removed her apron and made her way to the living room to do some last minute picking up. She had just selected some classical music to play in the background when she heard a knock at the door.

Glancing again at the clock, she furrowed her brow. Matt was awfully early. Then she grinned. Maybe he was just too excited to wait. The thought almost made her giggle. As she crossed the room, she straightened her top and ran her fingers through her hair, which she had again left loose down her back (but NOT because Matt liked it. Yeah, right) to straighten it.

She opened the door sporting a big smile, but the smile died instantly. It wasn't Matt at the door. It was her worst nightmare.

9

Altercation

Katie tried to close the door, but he was too fast and too strong for her and pushed his way in. Her fear spiked horribly, and she backed away from him, looking frantically for a weapon she could use against him.

"What do you want?"

The man answered her almost conversationally, "I want to see my son."

"He's not here, so leave."

Tyler's father gave her a nasty smile. "Is that any way to talk to me, Katie? You haven't seen me in years. Aren't you going to ask how I've been?"

Katie's former stepfather was well-dressed in slacks and a light blue dress shirt with polished black shoes. His blond hair was cropped close to his head, and he was clean shaven. Some might consider him handsome, but only if they were too blind to see the cruelty in his eyes. She had never understood what her mother saw in him. It had been four years of hell for all of them.

Katie was still searching for something to hit him with, if it came to that, and was contemplating if she was strong enough to lift the lamp when he spoke again.

"So where is Tyler?" He looked around the small apartment as he asked.

"What do you want with him anyway? You didn't want him when Mom died, remember?"

"Maybe I want him back. Raise him like a man instead of the pussy you and your mother have probably turned him into."

Katie was closer to the lamp now, and it was almost within reach. "Just leave. He's not here. You can't possibly want anything with me."

"Come on, Katie, honey. You're not making this a happy reunion for us. Maybe I want to talk to you. I heard about your mother. That's real sad."

She glared at his fake sympathy and refused to let him tear open that wound. She changed the subject instead.

"Why are you here?"

He shrugged and dismissed her question. "I wanted to see how you were doing." His tone turned taunting. "So did you miss me?"

She silently cursed him but refused to give him the satisfaction of a reply. She just wanted him to leave, to get back out of their lives and stay gone. She remained silent and gauged the distance to the lamp. If he came at her, she would fight him.

"So where's my son?" he asked again, taking another step closer.

"He's at a friend's."

"I'll just wait here until he gets back."

"He's not coming home tonight. It's a sleepover. So just leave, Jack."

"I'm not going anywhere until I see my son. I bet you're lying just to get rid of me. You always were causing trouble, getting in between me and your mother. You always were a lying little bitch."

He took another step and Katie was terrified and just about to dive for the lamp, when she heard a man's voice from across the room.

"I believe the lady asked you to leave."

Jack swung around to face Matt. He was standing just inside the door, feet spread slightly, and although his arms were crossed casually in front of him, the look on his face was far from casual. His jaw was clenched, and his eyes pinned Jack with a deadly stare.

Jack's posture changed. He stood up straight and eyed Matt warily. "Well, well. What do we have here?"

"Get out now, or I'm going to toss you out on your ass. And I'll enjoy it, believe me."

Jack turned back to Katie with a sneer and practically spat at her, "I see you've gone and got yourself a rich boyfriend, eh Katie? Putting out to get what you want?"

Katie flinched at the words but didn't speak. Matt spoke again, his tone deadly this time. "Get the hell out before I give in to my urge to beat the shit out of you."

Jack glanced at Katie, who was looking more confident since Matt had arrived, and then back at Matt. He guessed that they were about the same height, but Matt was more muscled and, Jack estimated, about twenty years younger. He decided he probably would not come out on the winning end of a scuffle. And besides, his plan didn't call for anything messy. No, looked like he was going to get what he wanted with very little trouble. He smirked, more to himself than the others, and turned back to Katie.

"You just tell MY SON that I was here, and I'll come back some other time. Now that I'm back in town to stay, we'll be seeing more of each other, Katie." The last statement was a threat, she had no doubt. A cold shiver passed through her body.

Jack walked back toward the door, carefully past Matt who had not moved a muscle, and out. Only then did Katie let out the breath she had been holding. She was trembling as Matt closed and locked the door before approaching her.

"Are you okay? You're shaking."

She nodded as he guided her to the sofa. Matt was shaking himself, not with fear but with fury. He had heard someone in the stairwell and had opened his door in time to see a well-dressed, handsome man heading up to Katie's place. He had stopped cold, seething with jealousy. His first thought was that this was what Katie was hiding from him. This man was her lover, or more appropriately, she was his mistress. He was obviously older than her and, judging from his clothing, had some money. Matt had never felt so much rage in his life. Katie, his Katie, who he thought was so genuine and so sweet. Some old guy's mistress!

Matt had slammed his door and went to the guest room to pack his clothes. He was done here, and he was going back to Boston tonight. He was so furious that at first, he didn't notice that the voices coming from the apartment above were not friendly, at least Katie's wasn't. He paused, one hand on his duffle bag, and listened more intently. He was sure now that he heard Katie say something about the man leaving.

Suddenly, his blood had turned to ice in his veins. Was she in danger? *Shit*, he thought to himself and practically ran up the stairs. The door had thankfully been left open and he could see Katie beyond the man's back. So far, she was not hurt, but she looked frightened, and he had cursed himself again for not responding sooner.

He now sat down next to her and grabbed both her hands, "It's okay. He's gone."

She nodded as if to convince herself of that fact. All the color had drained from her face, Matt observed. *Damn, what kind of asshole was this guy anyway?*

"Do you want anything? A drink of water?"

"No, don't leave me," she pleaded as she grabbed his hands.

"Okay, I won't. I promise."

They sat there in silence for several minutes and finally her breathing began to return to normal. He relaxed a little as well. When he felt she was calm enough, he asked her, "Who was that Katie?"

"Jack," she answered numbly.

"Who is Jack? Is he your lover?"

That got her attention. Her eyes snapped up to his and her face showed a look of horror and repulsion. "Good God, no! What would make you think that? He's old enough to be my father. In fact, he was my step-father for four years."

Matt had never been so relieved in his life. He mentally berated himself again for jumping to conclusions.

"What was he doing here? You never mentioned him before, so obviously you're not on good terms."

"He wanted to see Tyler."

"Who's Tyler?"

She turned to the end table next to them and picked up a photo of her, smiling, with her arm around a blonde headed boy, perhaps ten years old. His first thought was that it was her son, but the child was too old for Katie to be his mother.

"He's my brother. Half-brother, technically."

A thousand puzzle pieces slammed violently into place in Matt's mind. The man had said he wanted to see "his son," who was Katie's brother. Everything made perfect sense now.

"Katie, can you tell me everything? Are you ready to?"

"Not just yet. Can you just hold me for a minute? I'm still feeling shaky."

He gathered her in his arms and leaned back at the sofa. She cried softly into his shirt. It felt so good to be held, to be comforted, to let go. Soon the floodgates opened, and two years of grief, pain, and despondency came pouring out. The tears fell steadily, soaking the front of his shirt, yet he just sat there embracing her and whispering comforting sounds and phrases in her ear. Finally, after several minutes, her weeping subsided, and he offered her his handkerchief.

She wiped her face and eyes, now red and swollen, and after another moment, sat up.

"Better now?" he asked tenderly.

She took a deep breath and nodded.

"How about a glass of water now?"

"Okay," she agreed, "and can you turn off the oven while you're in there?"

A moment later he emerged from the kitchen carrying the water and she drank a little before taking another deep breath.

"I suppose you would like to know what's going on?" she asked with a weak smile.

"Well, I do, but only if you're ready to talk."

"I am. Thank you for being here."

"You're welcome."

They sat on the sofa, his arm around her shoulders, his other hand linked with hers, and she gathered her courage and called to mind the scenes she had tried so hard to forget.

Ten-year-old Katie sat quietly on the sofa waiting for her mom's new boyfriend to come for dinner. He seemed to make her mother very happy. She had been singing and smiling the last few days, so Katie figured he must be very nice.

The doorbell rang and Katie stood up nervously just as her mom came from the kitchen.

"That must be him! I can't wait for you two to meet."

Katie's mother opened the door with a bright smile, "Hi, I'm so glad you're here. Come in. Jack, this is my daugh-

ter, Katie. Katie, this is Jack, my… boyfriend I was telling you about."

Katie mumbled a hello. Jack said with a smile, "Nice to meet you, Katie. I've heard a lot about you. Your mom says you are very smart and do well at school."

"I guess," Katie said.

"Dinner is ready, so we can eat anytime," said Katie's mother. "I hope you like pasta."

"I'm sure anything you cook will be wonderful, Sarah," said Jack with a smile.

❧

Katie was curled up on the sofa doing her homework when Jack stumbled in the door. He made so much noise that it startled her enough to stand. She could tell right away he was drunk, could smell the alcohol from several feet away. She stood there staring, not sure what to do. He clumsily closed the door and looked at her before growling, "What the hell are you looking at, kid?"

She mumbled, "Nothing," and sat back down but her heart was thudding in her chest.

❧

Eleven-year-old Katie was sleeping soundly in her bed when yelling roused her from her sleep. "Jesus, Sarah. Can't you keep that baby quiet? Just feed him or change him for Christ's sake. Why does he have to cry all night? I've got to work in the morning, you know. Someone has to pay the fucking bills."

Katie could hear her mother's voice but couldn't make out the words. She held her breath, hoping that Jack would stop yelling.

"I don't care what the fuck you do. Just keep him quiet so I can sleep."

More mumbling from her mother. Katie stayed awake for a while, staring into the dark, listening for any more trouble.

✦

Katie came home from school and her mom was sitting on the sofa, looking blankly off into the distance. Katie immediately knew something was wrong. She dropped her backpack by the door and made her way to her mother.

"Hi, Mom."

Her mother turned her head and Katie gasped. There was a bruise on the side of her mom's face, near her eye and cheek.

"Mom! What happened?"

"It was nothing, sweetie. I… I fell." Katie didn't believe her but didn't dare call her a liar. Her mom pulled her in for a hug.

"Does it hurt really bad?" Katie asked quietly.

"It hurts some. I'll be okay." They sat for a while on the sofa, holding each other.

✦

Twelve-year-old Katie was helping her mother get dinner ready. They were having baked chicken, and Katie was cutting up vegetables for a salad. Her little brother was crawling around the kitchen, and she and her mother were keeping an eye on him while preparing the food.

Jack came in through the doorway, looking pissed off. Katie stiffened, immediately sensing that this would not be a good night.

"When's dinner going to be ready? I'm hungry," he growled without greeting.

Katie's mom responded with fake cheeriness, "Just about ten minutes."

He grumbled a response and grabbed a beer from the refrigerator. Katie went back to chopping vegetables, but now she was on edge. That was what Jack's presence always did to her, made her nervous and scared, never knowing what was going to be the thing that set him off this time.

"Jesus, Sarah, what the fuck does he have?" Katie and her mother both whirled around, suddenly afraid. Tyler had managed to open a low cabinet, had grabbed a box of cereal from the shelf and had dumped cheerios all over the floor. Jack lost it. He bounded over to the toddler and roughly grabbed him in both hands.

"No, don't get into that you little shit." Katie watched in horror as he shook her brother's tiny form, and she was filled with rage. She closed the distance to them in a flash and grabbed Tyler away.

She held him on one hip, while her other hand grasped her tiny brother's head protectively. She screamed at Jack, "Don't do that! Leave him alone! He's just a baby!"

"Don't talk to me like that you little bitch," Jack said menacingly just before his hand came crashing into her cheek. Katie, still holding Tyler, stumbled. Her back hit roughly against the counter but she managed to steady herself and stay on her feet. She could not believe he had hit her and while she was holding Tyler too.

She opened her mouth to scream again when her mother quickly grabbed Tyler and pulled the sleeve of Katie's shirt. She dragged her daughter into the next room and told her to be quiet. Katie was so angry her face was red and hot, and her fists were clenched.

"Mom, didn't you see that? Didn't you see what he did?" Tyler was crying by now and her mother was rocking him and making shushing sounds. Katie wasn't quite sure if they were directed toward her or her brother.

Katie was incensed. "How can you let him do that? Why don't you do something? We need to leave. We need to get away from him! Mom, are you listening? We have to leave!"

Her mother said simply, "Go to your room, Katie," and that was it. Nothing more. Katie had never been so angry. How could her mother let that happen? How could she let that monster hurt her children and just take it? Katie stomped up the stairs and into her room, slamming the door behind her. She threw herself face down on her bed and sobbed.

<hr/>

Fourteen-year-old Katie came home from her friend's house to find everything eerily quiet. She dropped her bag at the door and yelled, "Mom?" No answer. She kicked off her shoes and peeked in the kitchen. It was empty. Something felt wrong, Katie realized as her heart started picking up speed. She made her way upstairs and could hear the tiny voice of her brother coming from down the hall. The door to the bathroom was ajar, and Katie pushed it open carefully calling out again to her mother. The door swung open and there was Tyler, sitting on her mother's lap, babbling as three-year-olds do.

"Mom?" Her mother finally looked up at her and Katie felt as if she had been punched in the gut. One whole side of her mother's face was almost unrecognizable, her eye black and blue and swollen shut.

She dropped to her knees in front of her mother. Tears were already streaming down her face. "Mom! We've got to go. We can't do this anymore. Please!" She pleaded and something in her mother must have finally clicked. She looked up at Katie with her one open eye and whispered in a hoarse voice, "Pack some things for us."

Katie jumped up to comply. She went to Tyler's room and hastily threw some clothes and toys in a bag. She did the same in her room, going as fast as she could out of fear of being caught. She cautiously approached the room her mother and Jack shared. She was afraid to go in at first, but the door was open, and she could see it was empty. He must have left after the incident. She grabbed some of her mother's clothes and exited. Back in the bathroom, she took a hold of Tyler's hand and helped her mother to her feet. They grabbed the bags, walked carefully down the stairs, and went to the car.

Katie calmly buckled Tyler in his car seat, Sarah got into the driver's seat, and they drove away from Jack's house for good.

◆—◆

Matt had tightened his grip on her shoulder as she re-counted her experiences. The thought of someone hitting Katie made him crazy with rage. He vowed he would kill that bastard if he ever got his hands on him.

Katie, now emotionally spent, mentally pushed away the memories that she wished she could forget entirely. "Jack was a horrible person. The four years Mom was with him were the worst of our lives. She finally got the courage to leave, so we did. At first, he was angry and tried to get us to come back. But then he met some pretty, young thing and left the state with her, not caring one bit about his child. That was nine years ago, and we haven't seen him again. Until tonight. I don't know what he wants, but he's not going to come anywhere near Tyler unless it's over my dead body."

Matt gave Katie's hand another squeeze and planted a kiss on the top of her head. "What about your grandparents? Did you contact them when your mom died?"

"My grandfather had already passed away and my grandmother had dementia, so she couldn't care for Tyler. The social worker found Jack, but he didn't want Tyler. He waived parental rights, which was a very good thing. So I got guardianship."

She took another drink of water and chanced a look at Matt in an attempt to gauge his reaction. He was looking at her with a strange mixture of pride, tenderness, and sorrow.

Matt thought to himself that Katie was a paradox. She could be fearful and vulnerable, crying on his shoulder one minute and then threatening violence to her stepfather the next. A young innocent on one hand, a worldly woman on the other. She had to be strong to survive everything she had been through in her short life. He admired her for her perseverance and her resilience. He wanted to protect her and at the same time let her fight her own battles.

"Katie, you are amazing," he said softly, pulling her closer and placing another kiss on her temple. "What you have survived in your life is more than a lot of people could have handled. You are a strong and capable woman, and I'm proud of you."

"Thank you," she said, relieved and a bit embarrassed by his reaction. "I've tried."

"You've done more than try. I'd say you've done well," he replied, resting his cheek on the top of her head.

"I guess," she conceded. "I've always tried to take care of my brother, to protect him. I don't know what Jack wants, but it won't be good. I'm scared, Matt."

"It's okay. I'm here with you. You've been taking care of everyone your whole life, Katie. How about letting someone take care of you for a change?"

"I don't need anyone to take care of me," she protested.

"Okay, then, to help you. Surely you admit that everyone needs help now and then?"

"Yes, I suppose."

She snuggled closer to him and wrapped her arm around his stomach.

"I'm afraid he'll come back. Will you stay with me to-night, Matt?"

He stiffened, wondering if she meant what he thought she just implied. "What about your brother?" he asked cautiously.

"He's at a sleepover."

"Yes, I'll stay if you want me to," he answered. *And damn it, I'll keep my hands off you too*, he promised himself.

10

Finally

While Matt was determined not to take advantage of Katie in her current emotional state, Katie had a different idea. She was going to make love with Matt tonight. She had just poured her heart out to him, and he had accepted her unconditionally. He had actually been there when she needed him – something she could not say for any other man. Even as she panicked and felt desperate for some way out of the situation with Jack, she hoped – or maybe knew – that Matt would come. He had appeared, looking both handsome as sin and positively lethal as he stood in the doorway. She knew she could trust him, rely on him, and that fact almost made her cry with joy. He was kind and gentle. He made her laugh. And she was crazy about him.

He was leaving town tomorrow, so she would not get another chance. She made her decision. Tonight, she would not worry about Jack, about Tyler, about anything. She would not agonize over things she could not change. Tonight, she would not think, she would only feel.

She reached up to run her hand through his chest hair peeking out above the buttons of his polo shirt.

"Matt?"

"Mmmm?"

"Are you hungry for dinner?"

"No, not really. Seeing that bastard and hearing what he did to you has ruined my appetite."

"What should we do?"

"Want to watch TV?"

"No, not really," she said softly as she moved her hand up toward his neck and ear.

Matt suddenly got the impression that he knew where this conversation was going, and he was determined not to let her make such a rash choice in the wake of such emotional turmoil.

"Want to go out somewhere?"

"No, I feel like staying home."

"Oh."

"Matt, I think I'm ready now."

He suddenly became very still. *Shit.* He knew exactly what she meant, and he wanted nothing more than to explore every inch of her glorious body, but he reiterated to himself that she had just been through hell. He decided to play dumb.

"Ready for what?"

"Ready. For you."

He swore his gulp was audible.

"Shit, I can't believe I'm going to say this. As much as I appreciate the offer, and hell yeah, I do appreciate it, I can't let you jump into that situation now. You've been through a lot tonight. You're not thinking clearly. I can't possibly take advantage of that."

She sat up to look at him. "I know exactly what I am doing. You wouldn't be taking advantage of me."

The look of determination on her face began to chip away at his resolve. *Shit*, he thought yet again.

Katie was going to make sure she got what she wanted. She knew he wanted to treat her with care like a fragile doll, but that was not what she needed tonight. She moved to her knees and straddled him as he sat on the sofa.

"Katie, what are you doing?"

"I'm making you an offer you can't refuse," she said with a small, sexy smile right before she put her hands on his shoulders and began to kiss him passionately.

Shit, Matt thought for about the fiftieth time. He was having a hard time resisting her. God, he had waited for this, wanted it almost from the first time he saw her, and now she was offering herself to him and damn it, he had to decline. Life definitely sucked sometimes. He gently pushed her away.

"Katie, I can't let you do this. You'll regret it."

"Matt, listen to me. I will not regret this. I've never wanted anything so badly before. I won't think less of you for accommodating me. I won't ask anything from you, but tonight, Matt, please. I need you. Please – don't say anything more. Please, just make love to me."

What little self-control he had preserved thus far crumpled under her pleas. She must have seen the acceptance in his eyes because she smirked slightly and bent down to kiss him again, and this time he responded. With one hand behind her neck and the other on her bottom, he drew her closer. She was encouraged by his reaction and began to run her hands across his face and through his hair. He moved his mouth from hers and shifted his attention to her neck, finding a sensitive spot that made her gasp. She moaned as he discovered the exposed skin at the low neckline of her top and moved even lower to lick the space between her breasts. He worked his hands under her t-shirt and gently pushed it up exposing her bra and stomach. His hands slid around to caress her back as his mouth lingered over the gentle swell above her bra.

After a moment, he worked back up to her mouth, kissing her briefly on the lips, and then lifted her off him. Her eyes flew open in protest, but he merely stood up and grabbed her by the hand, saying only, "Bedroom." She nodded with understanding and led him through the apartment to her room in the back. At the foot of the bed, she turned to face him, and he came to her with more urgency now, quickly pulling her t-shirt over her head, running his hands up her arms and all over her back, and finally, releasing her bra. His kisses traveled down her neck as he gently pushed the straps from her shoulders, letting the garment fall to the floor. With more urgency now, she grabbed at his shirt and pulled it from the waist of his jeans and then, breaking contact for a moment, lifted it off over his head.

He pulled her to him again, and she sighed softly as she felt the intimacy of the skin-on-skin contact. She was aware of nothing but Matt's body pressed against her own, Matt's lips on hers, Matt's hand rising to cup her breast. He reached down to release the button at her waist and used both hands to drag her pants over her hips. She stood there, wearing only panties, as he slid one hand beneath them to cup her bottom. At the same time, his mouth moved to suckle her breast. She heard herself moan out loud, drawing a satisfied grin from him as he pushed her down on the bed, lowering himself with her.

"You're so beautiful," he whispered, lowering himself beside her and continuing his attention to her breasts. He moved lower to her ribs, to her stomach, past her belly button. Katie was now breathing hard and crazy with anticipation, every nerve ending on her skin prickling and alive. Every touch of his hand, of his lips, felt like a firebrand on her skin. She could feel her desire mounting, her need building.

When his lips left her skin, her eyes opened to find him watching her with an unreadable look. He paused to drink in the sight of her, her eyelids heavy, her hair tangled, her skin flushed. He thought that he had never seen any sight so gorgeous in all of his life. She wondered briefly why he had stopped, but then he started moving his hand up her bare leg, gently stroking her inner thighs, and she suddenly found thinking too difficult a task. He shifted his body and their mouths connected again, this time with increased urgency.

Slowly, his hands moved across her skin, sending shivers up and down her spine, making her wish he would end this torment and take her at once. Finally, he halted his teasing and paused to ask again, "Are you sure, Katie?" She whispered back, "Yes. God yes!" He kissed her mouth again and at the same time reached into her panties. His fingers found what they sought, and Katie gasped softly as they started working their magic. His gentle caresses and his expert kisses had Katie desperate with passion, raging with need. Her heart was pounding, and her skin was on fire. Tiny moans were escaping from her throat. She couldn't take any more, she realized, it had to be now.

As if he sensed her thoughts, Matt tore his lips from her mouth and blazed a trail of quick kisses down her torso. He quickly removed her panties and found her with his mouth. She gasped as a jolt shot through her body. The gentle rhythm of his tongue was taking her closer and closer to the edge. She had never experienced such exquisite torture in all of her life. When she finally found her release, the spasms that rocked her body were violent and she raised her hips off the mattress and grabbed at the sheets with her hands, saying his name over and over again until the tremors subsided.

He stood and quickly removed his jeans and boxers, grabbing a condom from the pocket before looking down to smile at the picture she presented, drugged and spent from his ministrations. Somehow, it made him feel satisfied, although he had done nothing yet for his own pleasure. She had no energy to move anything except her eyes, which took in every detail of his body, from his muscular things to his impressive six pack, to his very prominent erection. It occurred to Katie that Matt was like a Greek god, so beautiful and perfect.

"Come here." She reached up to him and he eased himself between her legs, but he did not give her what she wanted as his mouth captured hers in a greedy kiss. Her hips rose in a steady rhythm of their own volition, over and over, and when she could stand it no more, she let out a ragged whisper, "Don't tease me anymore."

"Are you really, really sure, Katie?"

"Yes! Please, now." Her plea was all he needed. He drove into her, and they both let out a moan of satisfaction. He started out slowly and tried to take his time, but soon she was dragging her hands across his back and shoulders, lifting her hips to meet his, and he could no longer think straight.

He rolled over onto his back, dragging her on top of him and pushing her upright to straddle him. When he grabbed her by the hips and entered her again, she let out a gasp that nearly pushed him to the edge. With every ounce of restraint he had, he forced himself to go slowly. She placed her hands on his chest and continued to moan and sign until he thought he would die from the sweet agony of listening to it. Yet he was determined that she should find release once more before he gave in to his own needs. Soon her gasps became more frequent and more urgent, and he too began to lose control. When she finally threw her head back, her hair cascading down her back, and called out his name, he allowed himself to find his own release. It was beyond anything he had ever felt before, and he was sure he didn't deserve to feel again.

Katie collapsed on top of him, spent and out of breath, her skin still burning from his touch. She snuggled her face to his neck and took a deep breath as his hands rubbed up and down her back, giving her tingles all over her still aroused body. Their lovemaking had been beyond what she could have hoped or imagined. She could not believe the power of her own desire or the depth of the aching that he had somehow managed to skillfully awaken and then quell. For the first time ever, she felt satiated, relaxed and utterly content.

11

Involvement

Matt was awake, his eyes open in the darkness, staring at the ceiling and listening to Katie breathe. Her naked body was wrapped around his like a pretzel, and he was far from complaining. It felt really good, really peaceful, just to hold her like this.

He knew he should be asleep after all the, *ahem*, activity that had gone on throughout the night, but he was restless and worried. He had planned to return to Boston tomorrow, but since Jack had threatened Katie and Tyler, things became more complicated in his mind. How could he possibly leave now? What kind of danger was Katie in? And Tyler? What if they were unprotected? What did that asshole want? And just how crazy was he?

Matt knew he couldn't just leave in the morning as planned, but he was unsure exactly what he should do. He needed to get back for some work things this week. There were important meetings that he could not miss. The first meeting was Tuesday. If necessary, Matt supposed he could stay another day and leave Monday instead. But then what? Katie and Tyler were still possibly in danger after that.

What to do? He thought it over and over in his head. And then when dawn was breaking, a solution finally occurred to him. Tomorrow he would make a call, and everything would be all right. Probably. And at last, he fell asleep for a few peaceful hours.

⇥⇤

Tyler was coming home from his friend's at noon, so at eleven, Matt reluctantly removed himself from Katie and her bed and kissed her on the forehead to wake her up.

"Hmmmm. Matt. What time is it? Where are you going?"

"It's 11:00, so you have to get up too. I'm leaving. I don't want Tyler to find me here."

"Mmmm," Katie softly growled in frustration.

Matt smiled a little and continued. "Hey, Katie. You know how I was going to go back to Boston today? Well, I think I'm going to stay one more day. I forgot something that I have to do tomorrow morning."

Katie looked up, still a little groggy, trying to process that information. However, she realized with acute disappointment that with Tyler coming home soon, they would not be able to be together today, and then tomorrow, Matt was leaving. *Oh, well,* she thought with as much positivity as she could muster, *I guess it's pretty much the same thing as leaving today.*

Matt asked what time Katie worked the next day, and Katie told him her shift was from 9:00 to 5:00. Matt promised to come see Katie at the bank tomorrow before he left. Katie figured that was something, though nowhere near enough. After planting another kiss on Katie's soft lips, Matt got up to let himself out, and Katie, unenthusiastically, dragged herself out of bed for a quick shower.

❦

Monday morning rolled around and after getting Tyler off to school, Katie readied herself for work and shuffled down the stairs. On the second floor, she paused briefly to look at Matt's closed door but decided not to stop. She was only going to get herself in deeper, and that was just not an option. Shit was already deep enough.

Katie entered the bank and greeted Maggie and a couple of other coworkers before going to her window to get ready for her shift. As she sat down in the place next to Maggie, Katie knew she was not going to be able to hide the events of the weekend from her perceptive friend, who seemed to be able to read minds or some such voodoo when it came to anything romantic.

Maggie took one look at Katie, narrowed her eyes for a moment, and then broke out in a huge grin. "Oh, wow! How was it?????"

Katie smiled back. "How do you do that??"

Maggie replied cheekily, "A mother always knows."

After filling in Maggie on everything that had happened, including Jack's unexpected visit and the general idea of what followed between her and Matt, Maggie became concerned. "So what does Jack want? I don't like this. What if he comes back?" Maggie's brain was working trying to process the situation as well as find some way to protect Katie and Tyler. She was really worried about her young friends.

Katie tried hard not to show the worry she was feeling herself. Now that she had time to think a little (because you know, there was very little going on Saturday night that involved thinking), she was nervous about that as well. She knew she would not let anything happen to Tyler if she could help it, but she was scared because she knew she couldn't defend herself fully against the large man. So she did what she had been doing for the last two years. Pretend.

"I'm sure it's nothing, Maggie. I'll be careful. He'll probably forget all about us soon anyway." she told the older woman with forced positivity.

Maggie looked at Katie with suspicion mixed with understanding and decided to drop the topic for the time being. That didn't mean, however, that she was going to stop looking for a way to help her friend.

Later that morning, Matt came into the bank. He had just finished meeting with a friend and so his business was concluded, and he was leaving Maine. There were several customers in line for the teller windows, so Matt busied himself pretending to look at brochures on certificates of deposits and personal loans until Katie was free. He positioned himself so he could see her because ... well, because he could.

Matt gazed at Katie as she interacted with customers. She was mesmerizing to watch. The way she talked to people, her kindness, her smiles, her demeanor — it seemed to light up everything and everyone around her. Matt was amazed, and very impressed, at the effect Katie had on people. He smiled a little despite himself, until a young, tall, well-dressed guy approached Katie's window. He was flirting mercilessly; Matt could hear from his current position. He scowled at the scene.

Maggie noticed Matt watching Katie and the cute law-yer and chuckled to herself. When Katie was serving the last customer in line, Maggie decided to take a break to go to the water cooler, which happened to take her right in front of where Matt was standing.

Matt was noticing this next guy, who might have been old enough to be Katie's father, was ALSO flirting with her. Did EVERYONE who came in here flirt with Katie? Again, Matt experienced a feeling that seemed all too similar to jealousy.

Maggie approached Matt and stood beside him, mim-icking his gaze towards her young friend. "So, I take it you're the guy from this weekend." Matt blushed slightly, chuck-led, and admitted, "I guess so."

"Matt, was it?"

"Yes," he extended his hand in greeting. "I'm Maggie." They shook hands briefly.

"So listen, Matt, you seem like a nice enough guy, but I sense you might be the jealous type, so I'm going to tell you something you need to know. If you're going to be involved with Katie, you'll have to accept that everyone loves her."

Matt looked to the older woman with some alarm, try-ing to process those words. "What??"

Maggie sighed, glancing again at the young woman with the blinding smile. "Everyone who meets Katie is drawn to her. She has that effect on people. If you're going to be involved with her, you should know and accept that you're going to see a lot of this," Maggie finished, vaguely gesturing toward Katie and the man who was clearly entranced with her.

Matt blanched, but he had no reply and Maggie was walking away anyway. He would have to think about that whole thing later. Matt chanced a look back at Katie who was finishing up with the last customer. When the final customer left and the lobby was empty of everyone except Matt and the employees, he approached Katie's window and smiled. She smiled back and he forgot for a moment what he was going to say. Mentally shaking himself, he told her "I'm headed back to Boston now. I wanted to tell you."

She smiled, perhaps a little sadly, and said, "Thank you, Matt, for the last few days. I had a lot of fun."

Matt suddenly looked intense and serious. "No, thank you, Katie. You made this whole thing… easier somehow."

Katie smiled a bit, but her smile didn't reach her eyes. "So, I guess this is goodbye."

"Unless I could… maybe come visit you some weekends?"

Katie smiled. She, of course, had considered this possibility but never presumed that he would want to. Hearing that he did made her feel all warm and gooey inside.

"I'd like that, Matt." He smiled back at her, grabbed her hand and planted a kiss on the back.

"I'll text," he said, giving her his dimpled smile and turning to leave.

Katie's heart stuttered a bit, and she knew her face was flushed from excitement knowing that they were going to see each other again. Her smile stayed glued to her face for the rest of the day.

12

Fallout

Tuesday morning, Katie shuffled into work in a bad mood. She had not slept well the night before, thinking about Matt and missing him. The last several days had been so nice, so refreshing. She had felt normal when she was with him. But now he was away, and Katie was in a crappy mood. She entered the bank without her usual cheery greetings and bright smile and mumbled a hello to her co-workers. Maggie noticed immediately and shook her head, afraid she understood too well the source of Katie's frustration. The morning progressed much like other mornings, and Katie managed to at least act a bit like her usual self with customers. She didn't know if it was habit or self-preservation, but whatever. Pretending was nothing new to her.

A little before noon, a stranger entered the bank. He was middle aged and in good shape, with brown skin, hair clipped short and beautiful white teeth. Maggie might have been staring a bit, so Katie smirked and excused herself to use the restroom in the hopes that Maggie and this new guy might have a chance to chat.

Maggie, indeed, thought this man was pretty damn attractive but, alas, at age fifty, it wasn't like anyone ever noticed her anymore. *Those days are long gone*, she lamented.

But still, she was old(ish), not dead, so she could look and admire. Okay and maybe flirt... just a little.

He approached her window and flashed those white teeth, and Maggie might have felt her heart skip like a schoolgirl's. He greeted her and pushed a check and a slip of paper towards her, saying "I just need to make a deposit." Maggie took the papers and said, "Of course. And how are you today?"

"Just fine," he replied. "Nice day, isn't it?"

"Oh, yes, a very nice day. So much better than all that rain." She smiled, handing him back a receipt.

"Well, have a good one," he said as he turned to leave. Maggie sighed again, admitting that was about as much excitement as she got in her life nowadays. *To be young again*, she thought.

❦

Wednesday morning, Maggie was practically giddy that the same man came back to the bank. He again approached her window.

"Hello. Back again today?"

The man replied, "Yes. Having trouble with my debit card. Oh, and I might enjoy the scenery." He winked and Maggie, doing her best not to swoon, pointed to the employee that could help him.

Katie was helping another customer but tossed Maggie a wide-eyed, suggestive look over the short wall separating their windows. Maggie blushed. *How old am I anyway? I'm acting fifteen, not fifty*, she thought to herself.

Not long after, a young woman carrying a courier bag entered the bank and approached the counter. She said to Maggie, "I'm looking for Katherine Williams." Maggie frowned slightly and pointed to Katie. The young woman then approached Katie and asked, "Katherine Williams?"

"Yes" Katie answered.

The woman nodded curtly and handed her a large yellow envelope. Then saying nothing more, she turned and left the bank.

Katie's brow furrowed again. *What the hell was this?* She looked at Maggie who just shrugged. So Katie opened the envelope to examine the papers inside. After a few seconds her eyes opened wide, and she let out a small gasp. Then she turned and ran back to the staff room without saying a word.

Maggie turned with alarm to lock eyes with Brett, the other teller, who had seen the whole exchange and had the same panicked look on his face. Brett waved Maggie back, indicating he would cover for them, so Maggie went in search of her clearly distraught friend.

"Katie, honey. What's going on?"

Katie was crying, sobbing in fact, curled into a ball on the floor with her hands over her eyes. The papers were strewn on the floor beside her. Maggie approached the younger woman slowly. "Katie? Can you tell me what this is about?" Katie still didn't answer and continued to sob, but Maggie was determined, "Is it OK if I read these?" Katie nodded, almost imperceptibly and Maggie gathered the papers and started scanning them for information. It didn't take her long to realize what was happening. Tyler's

father wanted custody of the boy. There was going to be a
hearing in a few weeks to challenge Katie's guardianship.
Oh, God, thought Maggie. *This is bad.*

"Katie, honey? It's going to be okay. We'll get it figured
out. I'll be here for you. It's going to be okay." After several
tense minutes in which Maggie just repeated soft assur-
ances and patted Katie's back, the young woman finally
stopped sobbing.

"Maggie," she whispered. "He can't take Tyler from me.
He'll hurt him." She let out another tortured sob as the
older woman pulled her into a tight hug.

"He won't take him. We won't let him. We'll figure it
out, Katie. I promise you." Katie nodded a little but seemed
unconvinced. She again whispered to her friend in a scratchy
low voice, "I can't let him get to Tyler. I have to protect
him! But what if they think he's better off with Jack? They
won't know about the abuse. Oh, God!" she moaned at last
and started crying softly again. Maggie tried to comfort her,
"It's going to be okay. We'll figure something out. I promise
you we'll figure it out together, okay? You gotta stay strong
for Tyler."

Katie seemed to stiffen. Of course, she knew the words
were true and it gave her a purpose. She had always stayed
strong for Tyler, and she would again. She simply had to.
Katie nodded and sat up a little, trying to reorient herself.

Maggie continued, "After we leave work tonight, we'll
sit down and make a plan. I'm going to help you, okay?"
Katie nodded again, a little more confidently this time.
She whispered back "Okay," and nodded a little more vig-
orously, if only to assure herself that the words were true.

"Just give me a few minutes, okay, Maggie? I'll be out there soon."

"Of course! Take as much time as you need," the older woman reassured the younger.

Katie was left to herself in the staff room and after another few minutes of trying to gather her courage, pulled herself off the floor and made her way to the bathroom to clean herself up. The whole time she was chanting to herself, *I have to be strong for Tyler. I have to be strong for Tyler.*

13

Plan

Wednesday after the bank closed, Katie and Maggie walked to a nearby cafe and sat at a table to discuss the developments of the day. There was a lot of talk and many tears, but they basically settled on a three-point plan. First, Katie needed a lawyer, and though she blanched at the idea, concerned about the cost, Maggie convinced her not to worry about the money now. That was a problem for later and was not important in the grand scheme of things, according to Maggie, and Katie grudgingly acquiesced.

Second, they needed some sort of proof that Jack was an abusive alcoholic. This was tricky as right now it was Katie's word against Jack's, but they both promised to think about how they could address that problem. And third, they both agreed with heavy hearts, that if all else failed, they would do anything to keep Tyler from his father, including arranging for Katie and Tyler to leave town. The two women were quiet after this discussion, each hoping it would not come to that, but they both knew in their hearts they would do it if they had to.

The lawyer was the first order of business. Neither of them knew of anyone locally that could help them, but Maggie promised to do some online research, and both were planning to contact people they knew to see if anyone could recommend a good family lawyer. They left the cafe with that plan in mind, and Katie had headed home to pick up Tyler and settle in for the evening.

After Tyler was in bed for the night (Katie had not told him about his father yet, wanting to spare him as long as possible), Katie concentrated on identifying who she could ask to recommend a lawyer in town. This was a bit of a problem since she didn't really keep in touch with anyone from high school and had gone out of town for college. Her college friends, including Grace, would not know anyone in Portland. And since returning two years ago, she had been painfully isolated from most people, friends new and old, with the exception of Maggie. She decided there were two people she graduated with, and one, unfortunately, was Ally Stanford, who she could ask to recommend a family lawyer. Then she was out of ideas, except for …

Unbidden, Katie's mind returned again and again to Matt. She typed a message and only paused for a second before hitting send.

Katie: Hi Matt, it's Katie. Hey, I wanted to ask you if you knew a good family lawyer here in town.

She held her breath waiting for a response.

➤◄

By Wednesday night, Matt admitted to himself that he missed Katie. A lot. He had been contemplating a long-distance relationship, and knew it would be hard but couldn't stand the thought of not at least trying to make things work with her.

He was also missing his mom, he conceded. He knew it would be hard to try to go back to normal, but he didn't realize just how hard it would be. It was easier during the day, with work and everything to worry about, but night-time was hard. At night, he was alone in his big and empty apartment with no one to talk to, and at those times it was really hard to avoid the realization that he was lonely, that he missed his mom, and damn it, yes, he missed Katie too.

He was sitting on his sofa in sweats and a t-shirt, scrolling through social media when he saw the text flash on his phone.

Katie: Hi Matt, it's Katie. Hey, I wanted to ask you if you knew a good family lawyer here in town.

Matt's heart skipped a beat. What? It only took him a few seconds to piece together what must be happening. Within 30 seconds, he was dialing Katie's number and was immensely relieved that Katie picked up right away.

"Matt. Hi."

"Katie, what's going on?"

"Jack. He wants… he wants custody of Tyler." Katie's voice cracked despite trying to keep her emotions in check. Matt closed his eyes, realizing his instinct was right when he wished like hell it was wrong.

"Okay, I know a lawyer in a really good family firm. When we hang up, I'll text you her information, and you can call her in the morning, okay?"

"Okay, thank you Matt." Katie's voice was a whisper and Matt felt his heart breaking from a hundred miles away.

"Katie. I... I miss you." He heard a soft gasp and a quiet choking sound. He waited for several tense seconds wondering if that was the wrong thing to say, if he had built up this whole thing in his head to be more than it actually was, then finally heard a soft reply.

"I miss you too, Matt." Matt let out a breath he didn't know he was holding. He closed his eyes and silently thanked the universe for those five little words. He wasn't quite sure what to say next.

"We'll get you and Tyler through this. We'll figure it out, okay? It's going to be alright."

"I hope you're right."

"I will be. ... I could come to Portland this weekend."

".... Could you?"

"I can, yeah. We can talk then and figure stuff out, okay?"

Katie took a deep breath. It sounded like she was trying not to cry again. "Okay. That would be... that would be really great. Thank you." Matt smiled slightly even though he knew Katie couldn't see him.

"So you'll call this lawyer in the morning and tell her you know me, okay?

"Yes. I can do that."

"Good. Okay. Well... I guess we should say goodnight."

"Probably."

"Try to get some rest."

"I'll try."

"I'll talk to you soon. Call me if anything happens. Promise?"

"I promise. Goodnight Matt."

"Goodnight, Katie."

They disconnected the call, both feeling a little lighter than before.

➳➳

Thursday morning, Katie took the contact information Matt had texted the night before and called the law office shortly after 8:00. She spoke to the lawyer, telling her she got her name from Matt, and briefly explained the situation. The lawyer agreed to help her, and they set a meeting for Friday during Katie's lunch break. She texted Matt to tell him about the meeting tomorrow, and they exchanged some cute messages that made both of them smile.

When she got to work, Katie relayed the information to Maggie, who was extremely relieved that Katie found someone so quickly. She also might have been a bit happy that Katie and Matt were planning to see each other again this weekend.

Friday afternoon came more quickly than Katie thought it would, and she was nervous as she approached the lawyer's office. She gave her name to the assistant and took a seat to wait for the lawyer, Brianna Jackson. Within a few minutes, a petite, pretty, twenty-something woman dressed in a dark blue skirt and jacket came to greet her.

"Katie Williams?" Katie nodded as she stood to greet the woman.

"Hi, I'm Brianna Jackson. Nice to meet you. Let's head back to my office, shall we? Would you like some water or coffee?"

"Water would be great. Thank you." replied Katie. Brianna led Katie to her office that contained, in addition to the requisite desk and chair, a small settee and two chairs arranged around a coffee table. Katie sat on one of the chairs, then Brianna handed her a glass of water and sat down across from her with a pen and paper in her lap.

"Okay, Katie. I know this is going to be hard, but I promise I will fight for you and your brother. But first I need you to tell me EVERYTHING." Katie nodded, took a drink of water, and told the young lawyer the whole story. It took almost thirty minutes, and Brianna listened intently, took lots of notes, and sometimes asked clarifying questions. When Katie finished, she was relieved that Brianna did the talking for a while, telling Katie about how the process worked and what her plan was. After that was all settled and they were getting ready to wrap up, Katie brought up the issue of payment.

"Ms. Jackson, I don't have much money, but I was hoping we could work out some sort of payment plan that I could afford." The lawyer looked slightly surprised.

"Katie, Matt already contacted me. He's paying my fees for you." Katie's eyes flashed with anger.

"No, I'm not going to let him do that. I will pay you. I just need a payment plan." Brianna sensed that she should not push Katie on this subject, and simply replied, "Let's just worry about that later. I'll just know someone will pay the bill, and I'm still going to do my job no matter where that money comes from. Okay?" Katie nodded again and rose to leave. Brianna walked her to the door and told her she'd be in touch Monday, but if anything happened before then to call her immediately.

Katie was a bit relieved to have the meeting over with but knew there was a long road ahead for her and for Tyler. As she made her way back to work, she tried not to be too angry with Matt for offering to pay the bill for her, but it wasn't working too well. Katie was more than just a little annoyed with Matt, and Matt was going to hear about it when he got to town tonight.

14

Reunion

Matt arrived back in Portland at around seven on Friday night. He dropped a duffle bag in his mom's apartment, thankful that he hadn't yet had time to call the charity to come take all the furniture away. Or could it be that he put that off on purpose just in case he ended up here again? He stopped for a split second and considered the possibility. Shit. Had he done that?

He pushed the disconcerting thought aside, eager to get upstairs and see Katie. Four days had felt way, WAY too long. Matt bounded up the stairs and eagerly knocked on the door. Katie answered not long after, and they stared at each other awkwardly for several seconds, not knowing if they should kiss or hug or what.

"Hi."

"Hey. Um, Tyler's here," Katie said, almost as a warning, as she opened the door and invited Matt in. Tyler was on the sofa texting on his phone.

"Tyler, this is my friend Matt I was telling you about." The boy looked up then and scrutinized the guest, who felt like he was on trial. Matt had never been good with kids and felt his palms sweat a bit under the boy's measuring gaze.

"Hi, Tyler. Nice to meet you."

"Hi," Tyler said simply. He was not too sure about this Matt dude. Katie really seemed to like him, but Tyler wasn't going to just accept him right away. He wanted to make sure Matt would treat Katie right. She deserved to be happy. He came back this weekend, so that was a good sign that he liked her a lot too. But still, Tyler was wary. He was going to watch Matt closely tonight to make sure he was as good a guy as Katie seemed to think.

If Katie noticed the way Tyler was assessing Matt, she didn't let on. She said brightly, "While I get the rest of dinner together, why don't you two get to know each other?" And then she left them alone. Matt's palms started sweating even more as he sat on the sofa.

"So, um, Tyler. What grade are you in?"

"Sixth," Tyler replied. "What do you do for work?"

"I work at a computer company."

A short silence, then Tyler asked, "What are your intentions toward my sister?" Matt almost choked at that question. What were his intentions? Did he even know? "I… um… I like your sister a lot." He decided to go with a safe answer, as safe as he could come up with right then.

"You like her because she's pretty?"

"Yes. Wait. No. Not ONLY because she's pretty. I like talking to her. And she's fun." Tyler squinted his eyes at Matt as if to determine if he was lying. Tyler was still glaring when Katie called them for dinner. Matt felt immensely relieved to be given a break from the interrogation.

The three crowded around the small kitchen table. Tyler was silent at first, observing interactions between Katie and

Matt. He smiled at her a lot, Tyler noticed. And Katie looked really happy as they talked and ate, so that was good. But Tyler still had more questions for Matt.

"Have you ever been married?" he asked Matt, out of the blue.

Matt was momentarily surprised at the off-topic question. "No."

"Do you have any kids?"

"No. I don't."

Tyler paused for a brief moment, then continued. "If you did have kids but you weren't with their mom anymore, would you still see them?"

Whoa, thought Matt. *This is some heavy stuff.* He sensed he needed to answer this question carefully and truthfully. "If I did have kids, yes, of course I would still see them even if I wasn't with their mom anymore. How their mom and I felt about each other wouldn't change the fact that I love them." Tyler's eyes, so like his sister's, held Matt's for a moment. Matt didn't flinch but silently willed Tyler to believe that he was a good guy. Good enough for his sister.

Katie was watching the exchange first with some amusement but then with some concern. This conversation seemed way too deep considering she and Matt had just started dating. She tried to change the subject.

"Who's hungry for dessert? I have strawberry shortcake." The mention of dessert had both males looking at her instead of each other. *Mission accomplished,* thought Katie, as she got the dessert from the fridge.

After dinner, they all hung out in the living room for a couple of hours playing video games. Around ten, Katie sent Tyler to bed. He, of course, complained that he was old enough to stay up later on a Friday night, but finally relented saying he'd go to his room, but he wouldn't promise to fall asleep. Katie rolled her eyes and agreed.

When Tyler was in his room, Katie and Matt snuggled on the sofa and began to talk. Matt started by asking about how the meeting with the lawyer went, and Katie described everything in detail. When she finished, she brought up what was bothering her.

"Matt, I appreciate you wanting to help by paying the lawyer fees, but I can't let you do that."

"Why not?" Matt was truly perplexed.

"Because. Because ... we're not at that stage of a relationship. I mean, are we even in a relationship? I don't even know because we haven't even talked about it. So you can't go doing something expensive like that."

Matt replied, still unsure exactly what Katie was getting at. "Katie, I have the money and I'm happy to do it. Why can't I help?"

Katie turned to face him and tried to get her words right. "Okay, so what if you paid all this money and then in a week or two, I didn't want to have sex with you anymore?"

Matt said with a confident smirk, "I don't really think that's going to happen, do you?" Katie laughed a little but was trying to be serious.

"No. I mean it. What if I'm like, I don't want this anymore, but he paid all this money for the lawyer, so I guess I'll just keep doing this. It's almost like you're paying me to have sex."

"What??" Matt was shaking his head, "No. No, not at all. What?"

"I know you don't mean it that way, but that's how it feels. So I can't accept it, okay? Do you understand?"

Matt's face was scrunched up like he was trying to work out a difficult math problem. "I ... guess I get it?"

"Do you really? I need you to understand. It's important." Matt thought for another minute how it would feel if he were indebted to someone he didn't want to see anymore. He thought he understood, but he still wasn't happy.

"I do. I understand. But I want to help you. I wouldn't expect anything in return."

"I know. But I would still feel that way. So I can't accept it. I'll work out a payment plan with Brianna, and it will be okay." Katie looked briefly at Matt but turned away again. She wanted to believe everything would be all right in the long run but didn't quite believe her own words. But hey, this was one of her specialties, right? Pretending to be sure about something she really wasn't certain of at all?

"All right. I accept your decision. But if you ever change your mind, you just have to let me know, okay?"

"Okay," Katie said with a smile. "Thanks."

"So, what do you want to do? Should we watch a movie or something?"

"Sure." Katie put on a random movie, and they sat on the sofa, but it didn't take long for both of them to realize that neither was paying attention. Bodies were inching closer, hands were roaming, and breaths were getting a bit uneven. Finally, Katie got up the nerve to turn her face up slightly toward his, and he bent down for a soft kiss, but then things got a little heated and soon a full makeout session was in progress. Before long, Matt had pushed Katie onto her back on the sofa and was halfway over her, kissing her neck and collarbone and moving his hands under her shirt and across the soft skin of her stomach and ribs. Katie had one hand in Matt's soft black hair and the other tightly gripping his bicep and was moaning softly at the sensations of the soft wet lips and tiny bites. Between moans and kisses were whispered phrases, "missed you" and "love touching you."

After several minutes, Katie let out a moan that was a little too loud considering there was a 12-year-old in the apartment. She realized what she had done, and her eyes went wide, and one hand went to cover her mouth. The noise also snapped Matt out of his daze to realize that this activity was not the best decision because before long, neither would want to stop. He took a deep breath and rested his forehead on Katie's shoulder.

"Katie. We have to stop... Tyler."

She scrunched up her nose, clearly not happy with that proclamation. But she had to admit, as much as it pained her to, that Matt was probably right.

Katie was acutely disappointed. "I've been waiting to see you all week."

"Maybe tomorrow you could get someone to watch Tyler?"

"I guess," she answered petulantly, sounding like a child who had been told she couldn't have ice cream for another 24 hours. Matt planted a firm kiss on Katie's lips and sat up, putting some distance between them, for safety.

"I know. We'll go do something tomorrow. We can bring Tyler with us."

"Yeah, I guess. I'm still not happy."

"Me either. But life sucks sometimes. I'll see you tomorrow, okay?"

Katie nodded as she walked Matt to the door. Neither slept particularly well that night, each of their thoughts filled with the other.

⤞⤝

Late Saturday morning, the three had decided to go to a movie that Tyler wanted to see. When they arrived at the movie theater, Matt paid for the three admission tickets without thinking. Katie was a little annoyed.

"Matt, I could have paid for Tyler's ticket. And my own for that matter."

Matt looked at her trying to figure out how that brain worked, "It was no problem, really."

Katie replied, "Well, since you bought the tickets, I'm going to buy the snacks."

"The snacks will be more expensive than the tickets," Matt noted.

Katie bit her bottom lip as she thought for a moment, hesitant to admit that he was right and that fifty bucks for popcorn and cokes was a bit too much for her budget. She suggested a compromise. "Okay, I'll pay for Tyler's snacks, and you can pay for your own."

Matt searched deep down for patience. "And what about you?"

"I don't want anything." To that, Tyler snorted, having been silent thus far through this exchange. Matt shot him a look, perhaps jealous that he himself did not dare to snort. He took a deep breath and agreed.

They got their snacks and Katie was actually relieved that she didn't pay for all three of them considering just Tyler's popcorn, coke and candy was almost twenty dollars. Geez. *Seriously, I need to buy stock in a movie theater,* she thought to herself.

The movie was somewhat boring for the adults, but they watched it anyway and held hands while they munched on popcorn and rolled their eyes at the jokes. It was a comfortable date, and after the movie, they went back to Katie's apartment and just hung out. Around five o'clock, while Tyler was texting with his friend Jordan, he asked, "Hey, Katie, can I go to Jordan's house for a sleepover tonight?"

"You were just at his house last weekend for a sleepover."

"I know, but I texted him and told him your BOY-FRIEND was here, and I guess Jordan told his mom and his mom invited me to stay overnight."

Katie wondered with more than a little shock if Jordan's mom was trying to get her laid. She chanced a look at Matt who was smirking and probably thinking the same thing.

Katie didn't know whether to be embarrassed or happy about the possibility. She turned back to Tyler.

"Well, do you want to go to Jordan's for a sleepover?"

"Yeah, it would be better than staying here watching you two make googly eyes at each other all night." Matt laughed and Katie had to grin.

"I guess that's fine then. Go pack and we'll take you over."

≫—≪

They dropped Tyler at his friend's house around seven, and as they walked back to their apartment building, they decided to grab a quick dinner, with an unspoken understanding that getting back and being alone was of the utmost urgency.

By the time they arrived back at Katie's apartment, both were a bit jumpy with anticipation. Katie went in first, and then turned to face Matt as he closed the door. Katie got a naughty gleam in her eyes.

"So, we're alone now."

One side of Matt's mouth turned up into a small smile. "Yes, finally." Katie approached Matt slowly and tangled her arms around his neck, pulling him down for a gentle kiss. They both sighed.

Matt looked down and said softly, "I was thinking, since we have all night, maybe we should take it slow this time." Katie nodded in agreement, because honestly, she would give this man anything he asked for. She allowed herself to be led to the back bedroom in a sort of a drugged trance.

Matt sat on the side of the bed and pulled Katie to stand between his legs. They kissed again, and Katie's hands went on their own volition to his raven hair as Matt trailed soft kisses across her jaw, to her ear and down her neck. Quiet sighs escaped Katie's mouth as Matt's hands worked their way under her shirt, over her bra, touching her breasts through the thin fabric. They had all the time in the world, and both seemed eager to enjoy every moment to its fullest.

After long minutes, Matt slowly inched Katie's shirt up and then over her head and then his mouth replaced where his hands had been, gently nipping at the pale skin above her breast. He reached to release her bra, then slowly his tongue flicked over one nipple and Katie's breath hitched slightly. She leaned down for a kiss, suddenly missing his soft lips on her own and then moved her hands to the hem of Matt's shirt and lifted it up, exposing the toned chest and abs. Katie then gently pushed Matt to his back and climbed to straddle him, pressing their chests together and enjoying the warm feel of the hard muscles as she leaned down to kiss his jaw and moving her hands down the long lean arms. Matt moaned softly as Katie found a sensitive spot on his neck.

Although they were both enjoying the agonizingly slow pace, Katie decided more skin was necessary and moved her hand to undo the button of Matt's jeans. She then unhurriedly inched the zipper down, little by little, drawing out the tension. Katie pushed herself up and scooted off the bed, drawing Matt's jeans over his hips and down to the floor. She was feeling pretty empowered right now and smirked a little to herself.

When she would have returned to her former position, Matt sat up and said softly, "You too." He placed warm kisses between her breasts and down her abdomen as he popped open the button and slid off her jeans to join his on the floor. He then moved his hands to toy at the back of the waistband of Katie's panties, moving back and forth teasingly. It seemed they were having a competition to see who could go the slowest and drive the other the craziest.

After what Katie thought felt like forever, Matt's hand finally slipped under the elastic of her panties to grab her ass and she moaned softly. Katie moved her hands into the soft black hair and pulled down gently, forcing Matt's head up and into another leisurely kiss. Time seemed to be standing still and neither seemed aware of anything except the other's caresses, breaths and reactions.

He pulled her down and onto her back and came down over her taking her mouth in a rough kiss. His hands roamed over her breasts and ribs as he trailed kisses down her neck, to her collarbone, and finally to take one breast in his mouth, then the other. He then worked his mouth down one pale arm, stopping to suck at the sensitive skin on the inside of her elbow, drawing soft gasps from her. Matt continued down to plant wet kisses on Katie's inner wrist and finally down to kiss her palm. Katie was practically wriggling from the sensations.

Matt was satisfied with his results and worked his way down the other arm, repeating the pattern. He then moved his mouth to her shapely legs, biting and nipping higher and higher until he reached the soft skin at the inside of her thighs. He spent some time sucking on that skin, relishing the lusty sounds escaping from the back of Katie's throat. Matt moved his mouth to the other inner thigh and stayed there until he was sure Katie could not take much more, then slowly moved to tease her with his tongue. Katie moaned again lewdly as Matt's mouth worked its magic, and it wasn't long before Katie was breathing hard and thrusting her hips upwards, before saying "Oh God, Matt, oh God... " and then reaching her climax.

Matt, feeling pleased with himself, moved his hand slowly up and down Katie's still sensitive skin in a gentle caress. After a few silent moments, Katie had come down from her high and was intent on returning the favor of that agonizing teasing. She worn a mischievous grin as she said, "Since you tortured me so much, it's only fair that I torture you too." Matt only raised one eyebrow slightly as if to say, "Bring it on." Katie smirked a response meant to convey, "You are going to regret that" as she again pushed Matt onto his back and climbed on top of him, whispering, "I want to touch you everywhere," and making his eyes flash with wanting.

Katie oh so slowly moved her lips from Matt's neck down one arm, making sure to run her tongue over all the muscled bulges of his biceps and forearms. She then grabbed the graceful hand and took two long fingers into her mouth, sucking gently. Matt's reaction was as expected, as he was getting really turned on by the suggestive gesture. Katie pulled the fingers from her mouth and smiled evilly, knowing the effect she was having on him.

"Turn on your stomach," she instructed Matt. He was a bit surprised but complied. Katie again straddled him, running her hands down the contours of his back. "Your back is amazing. Ever since the first time I saw it, I just …" She bent down to plant kisses over Matt's shoulder blades and down his back, making sure to work her tongue into all the grooves and crevices. As her mouth reached the waistband of his boxer shorts, she whispered, "Can I take these off?" Getting approval, Katie slowly worked the boxers down over Matt's perfect ass.

"Your ass is amazing. Can I bite it?"

Surprised by the request, Matt replied, "Um… I guess?" with his voice muffled by the bed. Katie slowly dragged herself up, purposefully making contact with his body the whole time, to whisper in his ear. "I'm going to need more consent than that, Matthew." That sent a tingle through-out Matt's body as he formed the words, "Yes, you can." Katie chuckled silently and worked her way back down to those cheeks. She concentrated on the left first, experimen-tally biting and sucking. After a minute she drew away and chuckled again, "Oh yeah. That's going to leave a mark." She felt, rather than heard, Matt laugh as well, as she moved to the other cheek to duplicate the treatment.

After Katie felt that was enough attention, she moved down one athletic thigh and stayed there a while because, *damn those thighs*, and finally, oh so slowly down the back of his calf. She switched to the other leg and worked her way back up, enjoying the sound of the ragged breathing from beneath her.

"Turn over," she instructed and when Matt complied, Katie straddled him and pressed their chests together, lock-ing their lips in another kiss. She was on a mission now and a bit more quickly than she had been moving thus far, planted kisses and soft bites down his chest. She lingered, placing long wet kisses all along his v-line, making Matt squirm.

Finally, Katie arrived at her destination and let her breath caress Matt's dick to get a reaction. Again, his breath hitched, and Katie was pleased at the power she wielded. With torturously slow movements, she moved her tongue over the length of Matt's cock before taking it deeply in her mouth. Matt let out a lewd moan and ran his hands through Katie's long luxurious hair.

She continued until Matt began to breathe faster and stopped her. "Hey, stop," he gently tugged at her hair. She moved his body up, again making sure to rub her breasts against his skin as much as possible, to finally arrive at his mouth for another deep kiss.

Matt flipped her over to her back and leaned over to grab a condom from his jeans pocket. As he slipped on the condom, Matt took in everything about her, from her long hair fanned out on the pillow all the way down to her shapely, pale legs and neatly painted toenails. She was trembling with anticipation as she felt Matt's long fingers start to tease her, so slowly and deliberately, as he watched her expression. She was so freaking turned on right now, she whimpered despite herself. Matt stopped briefly,

"Is it okay?"

"Yes …. don't stop," Katie breathed out a strangled response. Matt smirked and continued until he didn't think he could stand one more minute of not being inside her.

"Are you ready? Still want to do this?"

"Yes, Matt, PLEASE."

Matt smiled at her insistence and eased himself in slowly, taking his time in keeping with the leisurely pace they had used all night. But when Katie started moaning softly and wrapped her legs around his waist, he couldn't hold himself back anymore. All of the control he had managed to maintain earlier suddenly disappeared, and his animal instincts took over. His thrusts got more urgent and sloppier as he reveled in the sounds and words escaping her throat. He finally felt himself close to release and was happy to hear Katie's moans get louder and more ragged, indicating she was close to climax as well. He let himself go and was blown away at the intensity of the orgasm. After a short time catching his breath and trying not to put too much weight on her, he got up to dispose of the condom and crawled into the bed, drawing her to him.

For a few minutes, the only sound was their labored breathing as Matt held Katie tightly. Finally, Katie was able to form words. "That. Was. Amazing." Matt smiled and hugged her tighter. "Yeah, it was." They laid there without speaking for a few minutes, relishing the pleasant sensations still lingering over their bodies. Katie snuggled closer into Matt's chest, and they stayed that way for a long time, not speaking, and eventually both fell into a peaceful sleep.

15

Persuasion

Sunday morning Katie woke later than usual and was more than pleased to find herself naked and practically on top of Matt. She smiled to herself, deciding this was definitely the best way to wake up. She watched him sleep peacefully, his hair sticking up in places, his face relaxed and handsome as ever. Katie sighed and planted a soft kiss on Matt's lips before rolling away slowly to get out of bed.

She went to the kitchen to start some breakfast, glancing at the clock and estimating that they had less than an hour before Tyler came home. While she was cooking the eggs, she felt a warm presence come up behind her and nuzzle her neck. A low voice said, "Morning babe." *Oh, yeah,* thought Katie. *I could really get used to this.*

They ate in relative silence as Matt read the news and emails on his phone. Katie was preoccupied staring at the gorgeous guy in front of her, wondering what this was they were doing. *I really like him, but I don't know exactly what we're doing. Are we in a relationship? Should I say something? Will I ruin it? Will he come back next weekend? Gah.*

Matt looked up to find Katie looking at him with a slight scowl on her face. "You okay? What's wrong?"

Katie looked back at her food and brushed it off, "Nothing. Just thinking Tyler will be home soon, and you'll be leaving for Boston at what time?"

Matt replied, "Late this afternoon. I have an early meeting tomorrow morning. I don't want to get back too late." He smiled what he hoped was a reassuring smile, and Katie just nodded. She was still debating whether to bring up anything about what she was thinking when they heard the front door to the apartment slam open and Tyler yelled more loudly than was strictly necessary, "Katie, I'm home."

"We're in the kitchen," Katie yelled, though more quietly. Tyler came in to find them at the small kitchen table and he narrowed his eyes as if trying to see into their souls. He looked like he figured something out before grabbing some food and leaving the tiny kitchen. If he did figure it out, Katie wished he'd tell her.

⋙⋘

Monday morning, Katie was sleepy and preoccupied. She had spent too much time the night before worrying about Jack. She didn't think he had ever wanted Tyler, so why was he trying to get custody now? It didn't make sense. She went over and over in her head, looking at it from every angle, and she just couldn't make the pieces fit. She had finally fallen asleep but hadn't gotten nearly enough rest.

So today, from her seat at work, she was yawning periodically and waiting for quitting time to roll around. She had just answered a cute text from Matt and was in the middle of a very unladylike yawn when she saw Maggie's new friend come in yet again. Katie looked over at Maggie and mouthed "Give him your number" but Maggie turned away and pretended she didn't hear.

This time Maggie's friend allegedly came to the bank to get a bunch of dollar bills for the Boys & Girls Club yard sale he was volunteering at. But Katie thought he was just coming in to see Maggie, or at least she hoped. She thought the two were cute together.

When her new friend left, Maggie was flushed and started fanning herself. Katie looked over the short wall dividing their windows, "Well? Did something happen or are you having a hot flash?"

Maggie looked up at Katie, clearly embarrassed. "So, I might have written my number down on his receipt."

Katie smiled brightly, "Wow! Look at you, going for it!"

That night when she talked to Matt, she told him about Maggie's friend and how adorable it was when Maggie gave him her number. She spent several minutes talking about her friend and Matt listened without providing much in the way of responses. Katie thought he seemed a bit quiet.

"Are you okay? You usually have more to talk about."

"Yeah, just tired, I guess," he answered.

"Oh, my. It's past eleven. I didn't realize. I'll let you get to sleep."

He smiled into the phone, and she could hear it in his voice. "Thanks, Katie. I'll talk to you tomorrow. Goodnight."

"Goodnight," she responded and disconnected the call.

After they hung up, Katie lay in bed staring at the ceiling. Matt's lack of conversation tonight made her nervous, as she tried to figure out how things stood between them.

She was feeling a need to define the relationship and wondered if and when she should bring it up. She decided to sleep on it knowing she wouldn't see him till Friday anyway. She yawned, turned out the light, and went to sleep.

⟡

Tuesday morning, Maggie trudged into the bank, just barely on time for her shift. Katie frowned since it was not like Maggie to cut it so close. When the older woman got settled in her chair, Katie peeked over the short wall to ask, "Hey, everything okay?"

Maggie looked up. Katie noticed she looked very tired. Maggie let out a yawn but then a sly smile formed on her lips. "I might have stayed up late last night...texting with someone."

"You're kidding!" exclaimed Katie. "That's great. Tell me all about him."

Maggie looked about ten years younger from the glow on her face. "His name is Stanley Porter. He has his own security company. He lost his wife six years ago and has two grown sons. The oldest is married and he and his wife are expecting their first baby. He likes Mexican food and watches a lot of the same Netflix shows I like. He's funny. He's also a big flirt."

Katie watched with satisfaction as her friend gushed about her new beau. She loved seeing Maggie so happy. She hadn't, to Katie's knowledge, dated at all since her divorce. It sounded like this Stanley guy was great and just what Maggie needed. It made Katie feel happy too.

"That's wonderful, Maggie. I'm so happy for you. Are you going to go on a date or anything?"

"Yes, we're going for coffee today after I get off work," she beamed. She and Katie talked a bit more about Stanley and their upcoming date until customers started filing into the bank and they had to get to work. They continued their conversation at lunch, during which Maggie did all the talking as Katie listened intently and chewed her chicken salad sandwich.

Maggie's minor obsession with Stanley was impossibly cute in Katie's opinion and she loved hearing Maggie talk about him each day. They had been on another date — this time dinner — on Wednesday, and Maggie wore a megawatt smile on Thursday morning.

Katie just said, "Tell me everything," and Maggie did. Katie wondered if Maggie's face hurt from smiling so much. Maggie was enjoying the company of a smart, funny man for the first time in several years. The attention from Stanley was making her feel young and alive again.

However, Thursday morning Maggie saw something that caused the smile she'd been permanently wearing to falter. As she walked into the bank from the parking lot, she thought she saw Stanley sitting in a parked car down the street. *That's strange*, she thought to herself. *If that really was him, what was he doing?*

She thought about it all day at work, running it over and over in her brain, and by quitting time, she had a hunch that there was something Stanley was hiding. She couldn't be sure, but tonight, she was going to get some answers.

❖

Maggie and Stanley were having dinner at a Mexican restaurant Thursday evening when Maggie decided it was time to get those answers. She had been worried for a couple of hours now, feeling almost sick to her stomach at the idea that lodged in her brain. She hoped it wasn't true but had to know for sure. "So, Stanley, I know you said you own a private security business. Tell me more about that. What sort of things do you do? Do you have a lot of employees? Is it exciting? Or dangerous even?" she added the last question with a pang of concern for his safety.

Stanley smiled. "Nah, not dangerous. Actually, I do a lot of my job sitting at a computer."

"Really? Like what sorts of things?" asked Maggie.

"Like communications, surveillance, background checks, and the like. Actually," Stanley continued with a bit of a frown, "Most of it is pretty boring."

"Hmmm. I would have thought security would involve more, you know, field work."

Stanley flashed his straight white teeth again. "You would think, but…" and shrugged. Maggie was not done yet.

"I do have another question about your business. Why are you following Katie?"

Stanley winced a little as his smile faded. "I don't know what you're talking about."

Maggie was not going to let him off that easy. She simply had to know. "Stanley, I know something is going on. You started coming to the bank right after Katie's stepfather showed up. I saw you sitting in a parked car, AND you have a private security business. I'm not stupid. I know you're following Katie; I just don't know why. Did Jack hire you?" The last question was said quietly. She was praying that he said 'no' because she would be sick if he said yes. She was really starting to like him but would get up and leave the second he confirmed he was working for the enemy.

Stanley looked hesitant but looked at Maggie with sympathy and just said, "Maggie, I know you want to know, but I can't tell you. Please just drop it."

"Okay, fine," she relented, a little too easily in fact, which made Stanley a tiny bit suspicious. But then their meals came, and they ate their dinner in an awkward silence. Maggie wasn't very hungry or talkative, making Stanley even more nervous. He tried several times to start a conversation, but she resisted his efforts. She had said it was 'fine,' but a man didn't get to be his age and not learn when a woman said 'fine' but meant 'not fine.'

Maggie had finally had enough stalling. She was determined to get answers. "Just tell me if you're working for Jack. Please," she pleaded, "I need to be sure my friend is safe."

"Maggie," Stanley said with a warning in his tone.

"Listen, I'm trying to get information that could help my friend. Tell me, or I'm going to assume you are working for that filthy son of a bitch, and I'm going to leave right now." Maggie looked over the table to meet Stanley's gaze with a fiery one of her own. She was deadly serious about leaving. She would NOT consort with the enemy under any circumstances.

"Are you kidding me?"

"No. I'm not. I don't play around when it comes to one of my closest and dearest friends. So spill it."

Stanley looked harassed and debated for a couple of minutes. He took so long that Maggie started to get up. "Fine. I'll just go then," she said, but Stanley gently grabbed her wrist again. "Please, Maggie," he pleaded.

Maggie looked down, still determined. "Stanley, Katie is my friend. I need to know what's going on. And honest to God, if you're working for him, I can't see you anymore." The set of her mouth and the frown on her face told Stanley that she was not bluffing. He debated with how much he could and should tell her, and after a pregnant pause, closed his eyes, admitting defeat.

"Fine. I'm not working for Jack. Matt hired me. To keep them safe," Stanley admitted.

As understanding trickled through her consciousness, Maggie's frown lessened, and she looked tired and relieved. She smiled a little at her hard-won victory and sat back down. "Thank you for telling me," she said quietly and sincerely.

Stanley just sighed. "Can we drop it now?"

"Not until I get the details. What did he hire you to do?"

Stanley sighed again and accepted that she was not going to rest until she got her answers. So, reluctantly, he explained what happened when Matt had contacted him last week.

Stanley was in his office taking a call about a background check. He saw Matt's tall form darken his door-

way and waved him in, indicating he could sit at the chair across from his desk.

"Yes. I'll email the report now. Yes, you have a good day as well." He disconnected the call and greeted Matt. "Matthew! How's it going?" Stanley stood, smiling, and reached over his desk to shake Matt's hand. Stanley had been a good friend of Matt's father, and Matt considered him a friend as well. Matt sat upright in the small chair while Stanley slouched in his large leather one. He asked Matt, "How are you holding up?"

Matt shrugged, knowing that Stanley was referring to his mother's passing. "About as well as you would imagine."

Stanley's smile turned serious. "If you need anything, you just call. I mean it."

"Thanks, Stanley." Matt felt grateful but to be honest, he didn't want to talk about his mother. He wanted to talk about Katie.

Stanley got down to business. "So, you told me the basics on the phone, but I want to know all the details now." He got out a legal pad and pen and leaned forward to listen.

Matt began, "My um, friend, Katie Williams… I'm worried about a guy who's threatened her. She has guardianship of her younger brother, Tyler. Their mom died a couple of years ago. Tyler's father is scum — an abusive alcoholic — and he didn't want anything to do with Tyler until a couple of days ago when he came to their apartment. Said he wanted his kid. I'm worried he'll do something stupid. Either hurt them or maybe try to snatch the kid. I don't know. But he's trouble, Stan, I know he is. And I'd like you and your guys to watch out for them."

Stanley had been jotting down notes. He looked up to Matt. "What's his name?"

"Jack Johnson. Jack might be a nickname."

"What's he look like?"

"Early forties. My height but lankier, short blonde hair. Didn't see his eye color."

"He have a criminal record?"

"I don't know."

"I'll run the background check. Anything else you can tell me about him?"

"I heard him say something about Jersey," Matt said then paused. "Stan, Katie is terrified. He was bad with the physical abuse. I don't want him anywhere near Katie or Tyler."

Stanley leaned back into his chair and folded his hands across his belly. "We'll take care of it. I'll put a guy on Katie full time and another on Tyler. They'll tail them. I'll get a third guy, probably Seamus, on Johnson. We'll get a tracker on his car, make sure he steers clear of Katie and the kid. Meanwhile, I'll try to see what dirt I can dig up on him, so we know exactly who we're dealing with."

"Sounds good. Thanks, Stan."

"Try not to worry. I'll put my best guys on this. We'll keep your girl and her brother safe. You have my word on that."

They both stood and shook hands again. "Please do. And keep me posted."

＊

Stanley reassured Maggie. "I have my best people tailing Katie, Tyler, and the stepfather. If Jack comes anywhere near Katie or Tyler, we'll know it, and we'll keep them safe. They're well protected, Maggie, I promise you."

Maggie looked thoughtful. "So that's why you've been at the bank so much? Because you're watching Katie, to protect her?" Stanley defended himself, "And because of you, honey," he added a little too sweetly.

Maggie rolled her eyes at the last part, knowing he wasn't serious, but then nodded, feeling satisfied with this new information. A feeling of relief washed over her now that she knew he was not working for Jack and meant Katie no harm. But she also knew that Katie would be upset.

"Katie is not going to like it when she finds out."

"You can't tell her."

"Why didn't Matt tell her?"

Stanley explained, "Matt thought that if he told Katie he thought they needed protection, Katie might worry too much about not being safe. He didn't want to scare her." Maggie nodded with understanding. Although she didn't agree with Matt's decision, the main thing was that Katie and Tyler would be protected, so she decided he could live with the rest.

"Thank you for telling me, honey. Now, where were we?"

16

Quiet

Katie managed to survive the work week, despite her jealousy over Maggie and Stanley being so cute together. She missed Matt. A lot. Even though they had been talking and texting throughout the week, it still wasn't the same as him being here. Katie admitted that she was not cut out for this long-distance relationship — or whatever this was.

She was also nervous thinking about the custody hearing coming up in a couple of weeks. Her lawyer was taking care of everything, of course, but she still didn't know if just her word that Jack was abusive would be enough. She mentioned her worries to Maggie one day.

Maggie reassured her, "It's going to be okay. I ... I have a plan." Katie was relieved and asked what it was, but Maggie was evasive and wouldn't give details. Katie decided not to press the issue at the time, but knew she'd be needing more information later. And Katie still felt like there was a piece missing. She couldn't help but think that Jack wanted something besides Tyler.

Friday seemed to take forever to roll around again. Matt was coming that night and Katie was anxious to see him. Matt arrived around seven carrying a pizza for the three of them and something behind his back.

"What are you hiding?" asked Katie with curiosity.

"Where's Tyler?"

"I'm right here. Why?"

Matt was grinning with self-satisfaction. "I remembered you said you wanted that new video game. So here." He held out his hand giving Tyler the game. Tyler practically shrieked with delight, "Awesome! Thank you." Katie smiled too. She couldn't afford the game and thought it was really sweet that Matt brought Tyler a gift. She placed a soft kiss on Matt's lips and said, "Thank you for that."

Luckily for Matt, Tyler didn't interrogate him over dinner this time. Matt seemed to have bought himself some breathing room with the new video game, though he doubted he could win Tyler over that easily. Throughout the meal, Tyler watched them a bit warily as if looking for any red flags. Matt thought it was sweet that he was looking out for his sister but also felt a pang of sympathy for the boy who clearly had issues with trust. Not that Matt blamed him.

After they finished eating, Tyler wanted to play the new game right away. The two adults watched him, but sitting on opposite ends of the sofa, since they were trying not to grope each other in front of the kid. The kid, however, was onto them. He looked up at one point and said "Why are you sitting so far away? You don't have to pretend. I'm not a baby. I know you're having sex."

Katie choked and looked at Matt, who was actually laughing. *What the hell? That's my baby brother*, Katie thought with some outrage. But Matt just came to sit next to her, and they held hands and kissed, but only a little.

They all ended up trying the game and deciding it was fun, but it was getting late, and it was time for Tyler to go to sleep. He dragged himself to bed but not without his usual resistance. Katie would be very happy when this argumentative stage was over.

Katie and Matt sat up for a while talking. They were holding hands and sitting close on the sofa. The discussion of video games led to talk about movies.

"DC or Marvel?" Katie asked Matt.

"Marvel, definitely," answered Matt.

"Me too," said Katie with a smile. "Favorite superhero?"

"Black Widow," answered Matt.

Katie laughed. "What? Is that because you like looking at Scarlett Johansson in skin-tight black leather?"

"Well, that doesn't hurt," teased Matt. "But I like that she is just a normal person, but she holds her own against gods and superhumans. She's smart and strong. Kind of like someone I know," he added pointedly. Katie looked at him thoughtfully and nodded but didn't respond to his obvious compliment.

"What about you?" he asked, sensing that he had embarrassed her a little.

"Captain America, no question."

"Is that because you like watching Chris Evans in skin-tight blue spandex?" Matt asked with a laugh.

Katie laughed too. "No. I think it's because he's so principled. He doesn't waver from his beliefs. But the muscles don't hurt his case," she added mischievously.

Next they debated Star Wars versus Star Trek; Matt was definitely in the Star Wars camp while Katie swore that Star Trek was superior in every way. By midnight, they had talked about several movies and books and then movies based on books. They agreed the book is always better.

At a little after midnight, it was clear that Katie was getting tired, so Matt reluctantly admitted, "I should leave now."

Katie did not want him to go. "You could stay, you know. Since he's onto us and all."

Matt looked at her with a bit of alarm. "You couldn't be quiet," he said matter-of-factly. Katie shrugged and tried to sound as uninvested as possible when she said. "You could stay even if nothing happens."

Matt smiled. "Are you sure?"

"He already knows, like you said."

"Okay then, I'd love to spend the night here." Katie let out a breath she didn't know she'd been holding and the knot in her chest subsided. She had been afraid of Matt's answer, wondering if he wouldn't want to stay if sex wasn't on the table, but this, this answer was good. They got up to ready themselves for bed, and they went to sleep snuggled up, both feeling content.

•—•

Saturday, they took Tyler to the arcade and let him play a bunch of games. Tyler seemed to be warming up to Matt now that the three of them had spent some time together. They played some games together at the arcade, and Katie caught Ty smiling at Matt once or twice. Matt buying Tyler pizza and candy hadn't hurt his case, she supposed.

Tyler was getting more comfortable with Matt. He thought Matt was funny and liked that he didn't get mad at little things, like when Tyler dropped his slice of pizza and Matt had to buy him another one. Matt also seemed to do nice things for Katie too, like offering to get her another soda when hers was empty. Tyler was still observing, but so far, he thought Matt was an okay guy.

After the arcade, they stopped at the grocery store to pick up some things Katie and Tyler needed for the week, as well as the ingredients for the night's dinner. Katie and Matt decided they would cook (or, as Katie thought in her case, try to cook) chicken parmesan. She wasn't so sure, given her limited skills in the kitchen, but Matt said he could cook decently and together they'd figure it out, so Katie relented.

Tyler was playing the video game as they prepared the dinner side by side in the kitchen. It was cozy and comfortable. They enjoyed being together, talking, joking, teasing. They both smiled a lot and maybe a few kisses were stolen here and there.

Dinner turned out to be a success, much to Katie's relief. She was also pleased that Tyler didn't seem to feel the need to interrogate Matt. The realization made her more relaxed since she wanted badly for the two to get along. If, for whatever reason, Ty didn't like spending time with Matt, that would be a deal-breaker for Katie.

When Tyler went to his room (NOT to sleep because he was NOT tired), Matt turned to Katie next to him on the sofa and asked, "Should I get going?"

Katie paused. *Did he not want to stay again? This was so confusing.* He must have sensed her unease, because he quickly added, "Unless you want me to stay the night again?" She smiled with relief. "Only if you want to. I know ... it will be like last night again."

Matt grabbed her hand in his and kissed the back of it, "I don't care."

She nodded, "Okay then, yes. Please stay." A little after midnight they settled into Katie's bed again, snuggling closely. Soon they both fell asleep.

❧❦

Katie was having a lovely dream, about sex, and Matt, and sex with Matt. It was a really nice dream, but maybe the things they were doing wouldn't exactly be called nice. She woke up slowly and still, groggy, realized that she was (a) clinging to him and (b) still aroused from the images in her dream. They were on their sides, facing each other. She looked up and found that with the light coming through the window, she could see he was looking at her.

"Were you dreaming?" he asked, though they both knew that he knew the answer. She blushed and felt immensely relieved that he couldn't see her face turn red. When she didn't answer, he persisted teasingly, "What exactly were you dreaming about, Katie?"

She was embarrassed and didn't want to answer, but he saved her the trouble of deciding by capturing her mouth in a soft kiss. She sighed into him and really, REALLY wished that Jordan's mom had invited Tyler over again tonight.

"We should try to go back to sleep," he whispered, breaking away from her lips. For a moment, she didn't move or answer.

"We should," she agreed, but then continued gazing at the lines of his face, bathed in shadows. *God he was gorgeous*, she thought again.

He was still looking at her, trying to gauge her mood and thoughts in the darkness, when she said, "Or not." He raised an eyebrow, though she couldn't see the gesture.

"What are you suggesting, Katie? Did you forget your little brother is in the next room?" He could hear the smile in her voice when she responded, "No. I didn't forget. But… we could be quiet, couldn't we?"

He chuckled softly. "Well, I think I could be pretty quiet but I'm not sure about you."

She protested, "I could be quiet if I wanted to."

"You could?" he asked, disbelieving her.

"Yes, I could."

He was definitely smirking now and considering the possibility.

"Yeah?" he asked.

"Yeah," she answered.

"You're sure?"

"Yes!"

Matt laughed softly at her insistence. His hands began to circle her waist and move around to her back. He leaned to her, "Well then…" His words were a mere whisper in her ear but were so suggestive Katie almost moaned already. Damn, this was just getting started and she was already on the edge. *This can't be a good sign.*

Matt began nibbling on Katie's ear as one hand reached down to grab her ass through her pajama bottoms. She bit her lip, stifling another moan, and her eyes fluttered shut as Matt's mouth worked its way down her neck and collarbone. Matt whispered between nips and bites, "I just can't get enough of you." Katie shivered again, feeling herself already wet wanting him.

One of Matt's hands brushed up Katie's back and into her long flowing hair as he pulled her in for a deep kiss. The smallest of sounds escaped from the back of Katie's throat and Matt smiled into the kiss. He again whispered in her ear. "Shhhh, baby." The sound of his voice and the feel of his breath sent another chill down her spine. She was already wondering if she could really do what she had said and be silent enough. *Maybe this was a bad idea.*

She soon was lost in his kisses and caresses and began to move her hand under his t-shirt to feel the hard muscles of his chest and abs. She pulled off his t-shirt and her hand went all up and down his torso and arms. She wanted to groan with satisfaction but stopped herself.

He next lifted her t-shirt up and over her head and soon his mouth was fixated on her breasts. Katie clamped her mouth shut, trying not to let erotic sounds escape, but it was so difficult when he was kissing and biting and nibbling. She continued to bite down on her lip as he slowly moved her pajama bottoms down over her hips and off her legs. His hand moved to cup her through her thin panties, and he realized with a jolt of lust that she was already wet for him.

Matt moved back up to offer another deep kiss and Katie nearly groaned at the skin-to-skin contact. His hand reached into her panties and found what he sought and within seconds she was already breathing hard and bucking her hips slightly, but still, managing to muffle all except the softest of sounds.

"Matt, please…" she whispered, prompting him to hastily drag the thin layer of fabric down and past her ankles. Before Katie knew what was happening, Matt's mouth was on her and she had to put her fist in her mouth to stay quiet. Instead of saying it out loud, the words rattled around in her head, *Oh God. Oh my God.* Within a few short minutes, she orgasmed, only letting out the softest of moans, though damn, that was difficult.

Matt chuckled and softly asked, "Impatient tonight, are we?"

Katie looked down at him and whispered, "Only because of you, Matt." The statement seemed to push Matt over some dangerous edge he didn't know he was skirting. "Katie," he groaned in a quiet, strangled voice. "Shit, what are you doing to me?"

Matt moved up her body and attacked her lips with a messy, urgent kiss, drawing more mewling from Katie. Matt couldn't help but say, "Shit. Katie, I need you to touch me now," and she immediately complied, running her hands and fingernails across Matt's back and then down to his shorts. Matt sat up, scrambled off the bed and hastily removed his boxers. He stood at the side of the bed and

Katie moved towards him, eager to touch and taste his hard length.

She used her hands first, but then got impatient and took him into her mouth. Matt gasped and whispered, "Shit. Katie. So good." She warmed at the praise and continued moving her mouth up and down as she grabbed at Matt's ass with one hand. Matt was thrusting his hips forward with both hands in that long brown hair, pushing it back from her face so he could see what she was doing with her mouth more clearly. A couple of minutes later, he gently pulled on her hair to signal he wanted her to stop and then he pushed her on her back and came down on top of her again.

"Katie. You make me fucking crazy," he said almost savagely as he slammed his mouth down onto hers and used one hand to grab her ass and pull her up against him. Katie agreed with the sentiment but was too far gone to form coherent words. She was lost in Matt's touch and the burning sensations coursing through her body. *More, more, more,* is all she could think, doubting that any amount would ever be enough.

"I need you now," Matt growled softly, making Katie almost moan with relief that she was finally getting what she was burning for. Matt sat up to get a condom and quickly put it on and came over her body again, kissing her roughly and deeply.

"I'm not sure I can wait," Matt apologized as Katie stifled another groan, making Matt's dick painfully hard. "Are you ready? Fuck, please say you're ready," Matt practically begged.

"Matt, yes, PLEASE! Now!" That was all Matt needed to snap the tiny string of control that was holding him back. He entered as slowly as he could manage, given that all he wanted to do was go hard and fast.

He looked down and saw Katie with her hands at her sides, twisted in the sheets, her head thrown back, the pale skin of her breasts glowing in the soft light and thought he had never seen anything so beautiful in all his life. Something inside of him snapped and he suddenly lost the ability to think. All he could do was feel the need to claim what was his. He looked down at Katie, who again had a fist in her mouth as she tried desperately not to whimper and moan, and the sight reduced him to only animal instincts as all coherent thought escaped his head.

Although still almost silent, he knew she was climaxing because she threw her head back even further and he felt her muscles contract around him. That was it, that was all he could take, and he finished himself with a barely audible grunt. He collapsed onto her, breathing heavy, his head dizzy from lust and lack of oxygen.

They both laid there for a couple of minutes, still in a haze. Katie started playing with Matt's dark hair and soon whispered, "You're heavy." Matt grunted and rolled onto his back, pulling her on top of him. He continued to hold her close, his arms unwilling to let anything break the contact between them.

Matt was aware of some odd feeling that he couldn't quite identify. All he knew was that had never felt this way before and whatever this way, it felt amazing.

Katie was also aware of an odd feeling, but unlike Matt, she knew exactly what it was. She had fallen in love.

17

Threat

As Katie dressed for work on Monday morning, she alternated between two moods: appreciation for the amazing weekend she had spent with Matt and annoyance that he was now back in Boston. She knew they would text and talk while he was away, but it just wasn't the same. Katie missed him and she admitted she was a little petulant about the whole job thing that took Matt away Monday through Friday.

She walked down the stairs and made her way out of the heavy front door, not really paying much attention to her surroundings, only to come face to face with none other than Jack. He was sneering at her.

"Hello, Katie," he said with obvious contempt.

Katie froze. She was terrified. She anxiously glanced around, seeing if there was anyone nearby to help her if she needed it. Besides a guy sitting in a parked car across the street, there was no one to come to her rescue. She swallowed hard. He was only a few feet away. He could easily grab her or hit her. She fought the urge to step backwards and tilted up her chin instead.

"What do you want?" She tried to sound defiant but didn't think it worked very well.

"My, my. You are a rude little bitch, aren't you?" She flinched from the insult but didn't respond. Jack continued, "I wanted to talk. See how you felt about me getting Tyler back. I bet you're excited about that, aren't you?" His sarcasm was dripping, and Katie wanted nothing more than to slap, or maybe punch, that look right off his face. She didn't respond to his baiting, though. She just stared at him, waiting for the rest. She knew there was more.

Jack seemed to sense that she was not going to say anything, so he got to the point. "I have a proposition. If you want to keep him, you can have him, as long as I get a little something in return." *Okay,* thought Katie, *here it is. I will finally get the truth.* Katie's blood was boiling, but she schooled her features into a blank slate. She couldn't let him get to her, to see that his taunts were working.

"What would that be?" she asked, almost lightly.

"Money," he answered.

Katie snorted. "That's funny. I don't have any money to give you. Have you seen how we live? Paycheck to paycheck."

"Oh, but your BOYFRIEND has money. A lot of it, in fact. He's rolling in it. So I'm thinking he could set me up."

"I don't know what you're talking about," Katie responded, her voice trembling a bit. *What did he mean Matt had a bunch of money? Did he? And how would Jack know that?*

"Your rich, CEO boyfriend. He can set me up real good. A hundred grand ought to do it. He pays up, and I withdraw my challenge to your guardianship. You keep Tyler, and everyone is happy."

Katie was equally confused and pissed off. *What the hell? A hundred thousand dollars? Who has that kind of money? This guy is crazier than I thought.*

"You're nuts. Matt doesn't have that kind of money. Only rich people would. And I'm not buying you off. When we go to the hearing, they'll see that Tyler is better off with me."

"Will they, Katie? Really? Who has more money to support Tyler anyway? I have a very good job at the paper mill. What about you? Minimum wage?"

Katie's blood ran cold in her veins. He was targeting the very things she feared the most. How did he always manage to spot her weakness and exploit it?

Katie raised her chin in defiance. "You will not get him because I'm going to tell them about the abuse. I'm going to make sure they know what a monster you are." Her eyes flared with anger.

Jack smirked and Katie fought the urge to slap him again. "Your word against mine, little lady. You really want to take that chance? I'm a fine, upstanding member of the community. Plus, I'm his father. You're barely an adult. And with all of your mental problems..." She gasped, understanding what he was implying. He stared at her menacingly while his words sunk in. He knew the moment she relented, the moment she realized he could actually have his petition granted. She faltered, looking for words to make him go away forever, but none came.

Jack continued in his mocking tone, "Tell your boy-friend. Once I get the money, this whole problem of yours goes away." He turned without another word, leaving Katie to stare, mouth slightly open, at his retreating back.

◆┉◆

Katied walked into the bank, obviously upet. Maggie was already at her station and looked up to greet Katie, only to see her looking white as a ghost. Maternal mode was immediately switched on. She jumped up and went to meet Katie in the lobby.

"Katie, honey? What's wrong?"

Katie looked at her and the fear in her eyes made Maggie blanche. "It's Jack."

Maggie's anger spiked immediately. "Did he hurt you? I swear I'll…"

"No, he didn't hurt me." Katie looked around the lobby. She saw Brett at his station, ready to cover any customers that might materialize, so she pulled Maggie into the em-ployee break room. Putting down her purse and taking a deep breath, she turned to face Maggie and told her all about the encounter. Maggie was bewildered as well.

"Did he say something about a CEO?" Maggie asked.

"Yes, I thought that was strange…" but then Katie paused. She thought back to Matt avoiding talking about his work. *No. It can't be,* she thought as she took out her phone. Her hands were shaking as she typed the words "matt stephens boston" into the search engine. Her search yielded millions of hits, top among them, pictures of Matt, HER Matt, and articles about his super-successful company and his ridiculous net worth along with pictures of him accompanied by several beautiful women. Katie gasped and looked up at Maggie with heat in her eyes.

"Son of a bitch," she said. She showed the phone to Maggie, and it only took her a few seconds to register. Maggie's eyes went wide as she looked back to Katie's face. Katie was angry now in addition to being scared. "Can you cover for me while I make a phone call?" she asked, and Maggie agreed. She left Katie alone in the break room. Katie dialed Matt's number, her hands still trembling with anger and fear. He answered on the third ring.

"Hi, babe. What's up?"

Katie took a deep breath. "Jack met me outside my apartment this morning."

Matt immediately said, "Shit, did he hurt you?"

"No. He said…" Katie suddenly wished they could have this conversation in person. "He said if I give him money, he'll withdraw his challenge to my guardianship. He said you… he said you were rich, and he asked for a hundred thousand dollars." She heard Matt inhale sharply. "And he said you were a CEO, so…" she paused, closed her eyes for a second, trying to harness her anger. "So I looked you up and… well, you know what I found."

She paused for a minute, trying to get her nerves as well as her anger in check. "So I'm feeling pretty angry right now. At Jack and honestly, at you too. This was a big thing to keep from me, Matt. What the actual hell? Not to mention, if you weren't so freaking rich, Jack wouldn't have even come back to bother us." The last was said with a sob that Katie hadn't managed to stifle.

Matt was silent, searching for the right words. He too wished they were face to face. He knew he had fucked up. He hadn't intentionally kept his job and wealth from Katie, not really. At first, he thought it was just a temporary thing between them. He was only going to be in Portland for a week, and Katie was a pleasant distraction. Then he would go back to Boston and never see her again. He never intended to pursue anything beyond that, so he rationalized that Katie didn't need to know the details of his life.

Somewhere in the back of his brain, he admitted that he should have been more forthcoming about himself as their relationship — however it was defined — progressed. But he hadn't and now Katie, understandably, felt betrayed. Yep. He fucked up alright.

"Katie, I'm really sorry. I didn't tell you at first because I didn't think we would have this... relationship. I didn't know we were going to be involved to this extent. I'm sorry I didn't tell you after that. I just... I don't know why. But I didn't mean to hurt you, and I'm sorry."

A few beats passed while Katie took in his words. She thought she understood his reasons, but it still stung a bit to find out this way. She didn't speak for a moment and Matt panicked.

"Katie, babe. Are you still there? I'm really sorry. You have to believe me. Shit, I wish I was there."

"I'm here. I have to go to work now," she added, suddenly needing some space to think.

"You're angry at me," he stated.

"Yes, but I have to think. We have to figure this out. I have to figure this out."

"We, not you. Call me later. Will you promise?"

"Yes, I will. I... I have to go. Bye Matt."

She disconnected the call, a thousand emotions whirling in her brain. She tried to shift to practical mode, to switch off her feelings like she had done so many times before. It took her a few minutes, but she finally felt like she had wadded up the emotions and stuffed them away into the back of her brain so she could function for the next eight hours. She didn't feel quite as angry anymore. She only felt... numb. Well, that was okay. She was used to numb. She could do numb. She straightened her shoulders and tackled the day.

—

Matt hung up the phone and swore violently. He really wanted to go see Katie, but with the acquisition negotiations going on this week, there was no way he could leave. He cursed every vulgar word he could think of before dropping his head into his hands in despair.

He wasn't in that position long before his phone rang again. He wasn't at all surprised to see it was Stanley.

"Stanley, what's up?"

"Jack confronted Katie My guy, Rocco, saw the whole thing. Words were exchanged, but he didn't physically threaten her. She drove off, and he went in the opposite direction."

"Yeah, Katie called and told me as much. Shit. He's asking her for money in exchange for dropping the suit. Well, technically he's asking me for money, I guess."

Stanley whistled. "Bastard. What are you going to do?"

"I don't know. I'm stuck here while these acquisition negotiations are going on. Katie and I will have to figure it out. Have you found anything in his past that we can use?"

"No. Sorry. Haven't found anything yet. Still looking though."

Matt cursed and ran his hand through his hair causing it to stick up in places. "Thanks, Stan. I'll talk to you soon."

"Okay, be careful, you and Katie both. I don't like this. I've got a bad feeling."

"Yeah, me too," admitted Matt.

❧

A short time later, Joe knocked on Matt's office door. "What?!" yelled Matt. Joe recognized that snarl as the 'something is going wrong, and I can't fix it' tone.

"Matt, what's wrong?" asked Joe as he closed the door behind him. "Did something go wrong with the acquisition? Shit."

Matt looked up slowly and Joe could tell he was very distressed. "No, it's not the acquisition."

"Your mom?" Joe asked softly, thinking that maybe Matt was thinking about her.

"No." There was a pause that lasted several heartbeats. "It's Katie."

Joe finally understood. He crossed his arms across his chest and studied his best friend from his vantage point across the desk. A small smile formed as he realized that his friend had finally taken the plunge. He was pretty sure Matt didn't know it yet. *Poor bastard*, Joe thought as he promised himself never to fall victim to that fate. Nope, for

Joe it was all light and breezy. No serious relationships ever, that was how he liked it and planned to keep it.

"Want to talk about it?" Joe asked. Matt nodded numbly, still looking a little shell shocked. As Joe sat across from him, Matt leaned back in his chair and ran his hand through his dark hair again, a nervous habit that Jessica had hated.

"Fuck," Matt said finally.

"That's not usually a problem," Joe replied glibly. But one warning glance told him that Matt was not in a joking mood. *Oh. So it's that serious, eh?*

"So, it turns out that I might have done something really stupid," Matt began. Joe snorted, earning him another glare from Matt. He managed to wipe the smile from his face and look mostly serious.

"What? Did you cheat? Did you give her a sexually transmitted disease? Did you — oh God, please tell me you didn't tell her you loved her!"

Matt's head snapped up, "What? What the hell? What is wrong with you?" Joe was laughing again. "Shit, this isn't funny."

Something in Matt's tone sobered Joe. "Look, I'm sorry. I'll behave. What's going on?"

Matt proceeded to tell Joe the whole story, ending with the part where Katie was angry at him for not telling her he was rich. Joe listened intently, asking questions here and there. Finally, Matt was done explaining and said, "So she's angry and I need to apologize, but I can't get away this week."

"So send flowers. Women like that shit."

Matt looked thoughtful. "That, strangely enough, isn't a bad idea." He took out his phone and made a note.

"All right then," said Joe, "so we're all set for the afternoon meeting?"

"What? I'm still thinking about Katie! I can't think about the acquisition now."

Joe fought the urge to smirk. Oh, this was rich.

"So you've apologized over the phone, and you'll send flowers. Then, you know, text a bunch and put hearts emojis. Women eat that stuff up. Then maybe bring her a gift when you see her next, jewelry maybe."

Matt studied his friend like he was a specimen under a microscope. He couldn't decide if Joe's advice was the stupidest thing he ever heard or the most genius idea ever. He decided to think on it.

"I can't get back to Portland until Friday night. That's more than four days for her to be angry and stew."

"I still think my plan will work. Just make sure to say sorry and shit like a hundred times. And hearts. Use the damn hearts, I'm telling you."

"Why should I take relationship advice from you, anyway? You've never even been in a serious relationship."

Joe pretended to be insulted. "Oh, that was mean, my friend." Then he laughed and spoiled the charade.

"You're a pain in the ass, you know that?"

"I know, but you love me anyway."

It was Matt's turn to snort, but he didn't disagree. "Okay, now about the acquisition..."

18

Decision

At fairly regular intervals throughout the day, Matt sent Katie texts saying he was sorry, and he was an idiot. Several of those texts had little heart emojis. Then, late that afternoon, a huge bouquet of flowers was delivered to the bank.

The delivery man looked around when he entered the bank's lobby. "I'm looking for Katie Williams," he said to Suzanne, whose desk was closest to the door. Suzanne pointed to Katie, and Katie simultaneously felt a little giddy at getting flowers and angry at Matt using them to soften her anger.

They were beautiful, she had to admit. It was a large arrangement in a gorgeous glass vase. The colorful display included lilies, roses, snapdragons and even some lovely sunflowers. Katie tried to remember if she had told Matt how much she liked sunflowers. She pulled out the card. It read "I'm so sorry. I'm an idiot. Please forgive me." Katie softened a tiny bit. It was a thoughtful gesture, but then she stiffened. She wasn't going to be bought off quite so easily. But the flowers were breathtaking, and she could enjoy them, right?

Katie somehow managed to carry the large arrangement to her car, despite not being able to see in front of her. She buckled the vase into the passenger seat and hoped the whole contraption would stay put on the way home.

Katie wrestled the flowers into the vestibule of the building after fighting with the front door. Seriously, Mrs. Napoli ought to have that fixed. She carefully ascended the stairs, one hand with a death grip on the railing and the other with a death grip on the flowers. She was starting to get a little peeved at the size of the arrangement by the time she made it to the third floor.

She found Tyler on the sofa playing video games. He must have only seen a huge flower arrangement with legs. "What the hell!" he said. The legs stopped moving for a brief second, then continued. Katie carefully put the vase down on the coffee table and pinned Tyler with a cold stare.

"Pardon me, young man. What did you just say?"

Tyler had the decency to look embarrassed. "Sorry, Katie. You just surprised me."

"Where the... where did you learn that language anyway?" asked Katie, knowing even as the words were leaving her mouth that she shouldn't have gone there.

"You almost just said 'hell' yourself. Geez. The kids at school say way worse, believe me."

Katie thought back to middle school and realized Ty was right. "Fine. But still, try not to say that stuff at home, and especially not in front of Mrs. Napoli, okay?"

"Okay. Who are those from? Matt?"

"Yes. How did you know?" Katie frowned a bit and looked at Tyler.

"Who else would it be?" *Who else indeed?* thought Katie. Time to change the subject.

"How was school?"

"Fine. I got a B on my math test."

"Oh, that's good. I know you were worried about that one."

"Yeah. Thanks for helping me study."

"Anytime, kiddo."

"What's for dinner?"

"Chicken."

"Again?"

"Yes, again. Any homework?"

"Just social studies."

"Will you need any help?"

"Nah."

"Okay then. Let me get dinner started and we'll eat in about an hour."

By the time Tyler had gone to his room, it was nearly ten o'clock and Katie was exhausted. She texted Matt to tell him she was now free to talk and moved into her bedroom at the back of the apartment. She closed the door to make it even harder for Tyler to hear their conversation and plopped on the bed. Soon there was a video call from Matt.

"Hey," she said.

"Hey yourself. You doing okay?"

"I guess. Tired."

"So let me say again that I'm sorry. I'm an idiot. I should have mentioned it sooner."

"Yeah. This is… this is kind of a big deal. I mean. It's a big thing to leave out."

"I know. I never meant to hurt you. Please try to understand my frame of mind. I just lost my mom. I was here for a few days, and I never intended to come back. I … I didn't think whatever we had was going to be long term. I didn't think it was something you needed to know."

"I can understand that, but what about last weekend? Or this past one? How about in one of the hundreds of texts or dozens of calls? Why not later, Matt? I just don't get why you kept it from me so long." Katie was getting angry again, thinking about all of the chances he had to divulge his 'secret.'

There was a pause as Matt tried to choose his words carefully. "I'm embarrassed to admit, but I was afraid. I … I didn't want you to like me for my money. Like Jessica." Katie's eyes opened a little in shock, but then she was angry again.

"And when did I EVER give you the idea that I would be into someone for their money?"

Matt closed his eyes briefly in shame. "Never," he whispered. "Like I said, I'm an idiot."

Katie just stared at him for a few long seconds. "I agree. You are an idiot."

"Are you still angry?"

"I don't know. Yes and No. Maybe there are some things I haven't told you either," Katie was a bit ashamed to admit, thinking about how she hadn't told him — or anyone — about her depression.

Matt looked a bit alarmed, "Should I be worried?"

"No. I don't think so. I've never told anyone, not even my mom." Katie paused for a second to gather her courage. "I have depression. Sometimes it's pretty bad. But I've never gotten treatment for it."

Matt inhaled sharply. That's what she was hiding. He could understand why she kept that to herself. People didn't always understand mental illness, and there was still a stigma attached.

"Okay. Well, we need to talk more about that sometime. When you're ready."

Katie nodded, feeling a bit relieved to disclose the secret she had kept for so long. "So what do I do about Jack?"

"What exactly did he say?"

Katie told Matt every detail she could remember about the conversation that morning. She made sure to tell him about Jack's veiled threat to tell the court she was mentally unstable. Matt sat, listening closely, his free hand clenching in anger in his lap.

"So, I'll pay him," he said when she was done.

"What? No!" Katie insisted.

"It's not a problem. I have it."

"Matt, I am not taking your money, especially not that kind of money! We've had this discussion, remember?"

"But you can't take that chance. You can't take a chance that the court will side with him. You have to think about Tyler."

"I am thinking about Tyler, of course I am," she retorted, a little stung by his comment. Her anger at him flared again.

"I'm not taking your money. I'm not going to allow you to pay Jack for me, for several reasons. It's wrong to pay him off, and I can't do that. I also don't want to be indebted to you, so it's a hard no, all around. I'll have to take my chances at the hearing."

Matt understood her reasoning but didn't agree. "Katie, are you sure?"

She swallowed hard, but answered, "Yes. I have to stick to my principles. Like Captain America. Right?"

He wanted so much to fix this for her. He could do it too, he could pay the money and make this go away. But she didn't want that, and he had to respect her wishes. It didn't mean he had to like it, though.

"All right. I don't agree with your decision, but I respect it. If you change your mind, let me know."

"I won't but thank you."

"So what now?" Matt asked.

"Now, nothing. I tell him he's not getting your money. And we wait for the hearing." As Katie said the words, she knew it was risky. Her heart stuttered a little as she considered the possible outcomes.

She really needed some proof he was abusive, but she didn't think her mother had ever called the police, so he probably wouldn't even have a record. What else could she do? How could she make this go away? Was she really going to just wait and see what happened at the hearing? Could she?

"Hey, it's going to be okay," Matt tried to reassure her, interpreting her silence correctly.

"I hope you're right," she said, taking a deep breath.

"I'll be back on Friday night, but we'll talk tomorrow?"

"I guess. Yes."

"Okay. Get some rest."

"I'll try," said Katie.

After they disconnected the call, Matt sat unmoving for several minutes, going back over their conversation. Hopefully Stanley would dig up some dirt. If not, he wasn't all that confident about the outcome of the hearing.

❖

Every time Katie left her apartment now, she was nervous that she would find Jack outside waiting for her again. She opened the big heavy door slowly and peeked around it, looking for any shadows or forms. She didn't see anything for the next three days, but when she emerged on Friday morning, he was there, looking as smarmy as ever.

"Hi there, Katie. Did you miss me?"

She stiffened at the sound of his voice, low and mocking. "Nope," she said simply.

He chuckled a little. "Well, that's too bad. So have you talked to that boyfriend of yours? You gonna do the smart thing and make this whole problem go away?"

"No."

"What?" Jack couldn't believe what he'd heard.

"No, I'm not giving you money. I mean Matt is not giving you money. I'll take my chances at the hearing."

Jack's face was starting to get red, and she could see the anger in his eyes. He was scary when he got like this. She was afraid to take her eyes off him in case he became violent.

"You're a stupid little bitch, you know that?"

"I've never cared about what you thought of me, and I don't care now. I guess I'll see you at the hearing."

She turned and walked away, leaving him glued to the spot. He couldn't believe she didn't go for it. When he saw Katie with that rich boyfriend, he could tell the guy was head-over-heels for her, so why wouldn't he pay? Son of a bitch. Maybe he overestimated their relationship. Or maybe he asked for too much? What was he going to do now? That little bitch always had made him angry, never showing him proper respect. He walked back to his car and contemplated his next move.

Katie was shaking like a leaf as she got into her car. She gripped the steering wheel tightly to stop her hands from trembling. She would not let him do this. She would not let him intimidate her, extort her, scare her. None of it. She was strong and she was going to figure out something to make things okay. She wasn't sure what or how, but she was determined.

By the time Katie got to work, her heart rate had returned to normal, and she no longer felt a burning rage in her chest. She was back in numb mode. She'd get through the day and figure things out later. She plastered another fake smile on her face and went to work.

19

Attack

It was Friday night around nine, and Matt was almost back to Portland. He had been held up with the acquisition negotiations and hadn't been able to leave as early as he wanted. He was eager to get back to Katie, to see her in person and explain how sorry he was. Hopefully she would take pity on him and forgive him for his screw up. He hoped she was the forgiving type.

⇥·⇤

At 8:55 PM, Stanley heard his phone ring and looked to see a call from Seamus. Oh, no. He picked up right away and growled "What?"

Seamus sounded panicked, "We have a problem. Jack just left his house, and I think he's headed towards Katie's. And he's been drinking tonight. He was at the bar for at least two hours after work."

Stanley cursed silently. "How far away?"

"Tracker says he's almost there. I didn't notice he was on the move. I thought he was home for the night. Shit, I'm sorry. I'll be there in ten," Seamus said.

"I'll call Rocco," replied Stanley as he grabbed his keys and headed toward the door. He dialed Rocco, who was currently sitting in a car across the street from Katie's apartment.

"Yeah?" answered Rocco as he sipped on some Dunkin Donuts coffee.

Stanley explained, "Jack is on his way there, we think. Seamus said he's been drinking so there's no telling what he'll do. I'll be there in five minutes. Seamus will be there in ten."

"I wouldn't worry about it," Rocco said calmly. "He can't get inside the building."

Stanley replied with urgency, "Well still. Let's be safe." He hung up and turned to Maggie, "We have to go to Katie's. Jack is on his way, and he's been drinking. I don't think they're in danger because he shouldn't be able to get into the building, but we're going anyway to be sure." Maggie looked stricken, but just nodded, grabbed her purse and followed Stanley out the door.

Rocco watched Katie's building closely and within minutes saw a newer model sports car pull up and park a little crookedly on the street. Soon a tall, middle-aged man exited the car, slightly unsteady on his feet. Rocco watched as he staggered to the door of Katie's building and then was dumbfounded when the man opened the large external door and just walked in.

"What the fuck?" said Rocco. The door was supposed to be locked. "Shit!" he said, quickly jumping out of the car and running after the man.

⇻⇺

Katie and Tyler were hanging in their living room. Katie had originally planned to cook dinner but was too tired and upset when she got home from work, so they had ordered pizza instead. Tyler had noticed that Katie seemed off tonight, but he also loved pizza so he didn't argue. Sometimes Katie got like this, all quiet and thoughtful. She probably thought he didn't notice but he did. He often watched and observed Katie. When she got like this, he wanted so much to help, but he didn't know how.

When the pizza arrived, Katie had gone down to the big front door to meet the delivery person. She was already in a bad mood so when the door stuck again, she threw her weight against it, taking out her frustrations on the inanimate object which clearly had been placed there by the universe to screw with her day even more. She had finally wrestled the door open, gotten their pizza, and swung the door closed. She had her hands full and was more than a little ticked off by the time she made it to the third floor. She had opened the door to their apartment and kicked it closed with one foot. "Tyler! Pizza's here."

Now that they had eaten, Tyler was playing the new video game Matt had bought him. Katie was just sitting in a chair, lost in thought. She was shocked when the door to their apartment slammed open and Jack sauntered in, swaying a little, obviously drunk. Katie jumped to her feet and, in a panic, tried to process the situation. The door to the building must not have closed all the way, and shit, she had forgotten to lock the apartment door when she came in with her hands full of pizza. *Oh no, no, no!*

Tyler scrambled to his feet, staring in disbelief at the stranger, not knowing who he was or why he had just barged into their apartment. Katie quickly jumped in front of him, placing herself between Tyler and the monster in front of her. She would NOT let this asshole hurt Tyler. She wasn't much bigger than she was at 14, but she thought she could hold him off at least somewhat and that would hopefully give Ty enough time to get away. And she would do everything in her power to make that happen.

Jack approached them on unsteady feet and slurring his words, hissed out at Katie, "You little bitch. You ruined everything. Why couldn't you just hand over the money like I wanted? Huh? Why do you always have to fuck things up?"

"Get out! I'm going to call the police."

"Who the fuck do you think you are, anyway? All high and mighty, just like your mother was."

She glanced around and noted that her phone was still on the chair several feet away. She couldn't grab it without giving up her position in between Ty and his father.

"Just go, Jack. I'm calling the police." Then she tried another approach. "You know, this won't look good for you at the hearing," she noted.

Though his drunk brain was processing information slowly, Jack seemed to realize that what Katie said was true. It sparked his anger and he suddenly wanted to take it out on Katie. He lunged at her swinging as Tyler screamed and jumped back in terror. Jack's fist caught Katie's face and though the punch connected (and hurt) it didn't have as much force as expected because he was drunk and off-balance. Jack stumbled and tried to right himself when he was suddenly tackled from behind.

Katie saw a chance to get Tyler to safety. "Tyler, run! Go to Mrs. Napoli's now!! Lock the door. Tell her to call the police," she yelled with a shaky voice. Tyler ran to the still open door and bolted down the stairs. Katie thought, *Please, God, let him get there safely.*

A dark-haired man Katie did not know was trying to restrain Tyler's father but was only partially successful since Jack was in some sort of alcohol-induced rage. Katie was debating if and how she should join the fray when Stanley came bursting through the open door. He immediately was able to help the other man subdue the assailant as Katie watched in shock. Jack was face down on the floor; Stanley had one knee on his back and was restraining his arms behind him. He and the other man were both breathing hard but appeared to be unhurt. A minute later, a red-headed man came running into the apartment but stopped short when he saw that Stanley had the situation under control. Within another minute, they all heard sirens close by and stood anxiously waiting for the police.

20

Confrontation

Within minutes, police officers arrived and began restraining Jack and gathering statements. Stanley knew the ranking officer, who promised to keep Stanley apprised of any developments in the case.

Just as Jack was being escorted from the apartment, Matt bolted through the open door and stopped short. He took one look at Jack and started toward him, rage in his eyes. Stanley and the dark-haired man each grabbed one of Matt's arms to restrain him.

"Matthew, don't. He's not worth it."

Matt swung around to face Stanley, eyes wide and skin flushed. He seemed to take a minute to process Stanley's words and then tried to calm his anger. After a moment and a few deep breaths, he nodded once, realizing Stanley was right, but boy did he want to beat the shit out of that piece-of-crap-excuse for a human being.

He scanned the room for Katie and saw her sitting on the sofa, holding Tyler close with one arm and using the other hand to hold an ice pack to her bruised and swollen face. His heart skipped a beat.

"Katie," Matt called in a strangled voice. "My God. Are you okay? Is Tyler?"

"Ty is fine. I'm okay, but my face..." she trailed off quietly.

Katie's face hurt terribly, but she knew the punch could have been much harder and much worse, so she was thankful for that at least. Tyler was clutching onto her tightly, having hardly let her go since he returned to the apartment. He appeared to be sleeping and Katie hoped he felt safer glued to her side.

Stanley and his associates, who Katie learned were named Rocco and Seamus, had stayed with Katie, along with Maggie, who had come up from the car after all the excitement had died down. In the last few minutes, Stanley had been explaining to her how the three of them had been tailing Katie, Tyler and Jack for the last few weeks.

Katie listened without speaking, not sure how to react. On one hand, she was relieved that they had protection when they had needed it. She would at least thank Matt for that. And now she didn't think she'd have to worry about the custody hearing, seeing as how Tyler's father had attacked them.

But she was also angry. Matt had done something without telling her, interfered in her life without her permission, treated her like a child who couldn't be trusted to make her own decisions and control her own life. She understood why Matt had done it, but she was still angry about it. This seemed like just another instance of him keeping things from her. How can you build a relationship when one person is always hiding things?

Matt approached Katie and kneeled in front of her. He reached up to move the hair from her face. Katie looked down, part of her relieved to see him even as another part of her felt anger at him for not confiding in her. Again.

She ignored his gesture and roused Tyler from his slumber. Ty didn't need to hear this after all he'd already been through. "Ty, come on, let's get you to bed." He mumbled a little in protest but went along with her to his room where she tucked him in and kissed his forehead, thanking God and the universe yet again for his safety. Katie returned to the living room and steeled herself for the confrontation that was about to go down.

When Katie reentered the living room, Matt finally got a good look at her face without it being obscured by the ice pack, and he became enraged all over again. He could see the swelling and the discoloration and felt like he could kill Jack with his bare hands right now.

His expression was pained as he closed the distance between them, "Oh my God. Katie, your face." He reached up as if to touch the bruise, but Katie swatted his hand away. Matt should not have been surprised given the way things stood between them, but he was anyway because that was so unlike his Katie. *His Katie? Was Katie ever his?* He swallowed with difficulty.

"I'm okay." Katie replied without much emotion. She resumed her place on the sofa, then continued coldly. "Oh, and thanks for the bodyguards. Wish I'd known about them earlier."

Another jibe. For a moment, no one made a sound and Matt looked nervously around the room. Maggie looked at him warily, which he understood since he hurt her friend, and Stanley and the other two men looked at him with some compassion. There was some movement as Stanley began to stand and said, "I think we'll be going now." But Katie stopped them and said "No, don't go."

The others looked at each other with uncertainty. Maggie asked gently, "Katie, are you sure you want an audience for this?" Katie shrugged. A few beats passed. Maggie continued, "How about if we just go in the kitchen? We'll be right there if you need anything. Okay?" Katie nodded almost imperceptibly, causing the two men to take their leave altogether as Stanley and Maggie headed to the kitchen. All four were relieved to not be caught in the middle of whatever was about to happen.

Matt knew he needed to apologize, to make things better, to say the right things to make Katie understand, but right now he couldn't seem to think straight. He began to feel anxiety and pressure rise in his chest. He had to fix this. Again. How many times would she let him screw up before she gave up on him?

Matt cleared his throat and approached Katie, who met his eyes briefly but then looked away. He sat down carefully in the spot that Tyler had recently occupied and tried desperately to find the right words.

"I know you're angry. Again. Please let me try to explain."

Matt's heart was thudding in his chest. He was so afraid of messing things up again. He took a deep breath and carefully searched for the words.

"I'm sorry I didn't tell you about hiring Stanley. I was scared that you would worry too much, that you would think that there was more danger because I thought you needed protection. I was trying to make things easier for you, Katie. You've had things so hard. I thought, this is something I can do to help. To make your life a tiny bit better. I did it for you. Not because I thought you couldn't handle it. Shit, I'm amazed at everything you can and have handled."

Matt paused and looked at Katie, trying to gauge her reaction. He thought, just maybe, Katie's posture had softened a tiny bit since he started. He waited for several moments to see if she would say anything. Finally, Katie spoke softly.

"I understand. You did that before we talked about the lawyer, before I told you I didn't want to feel like I was obligated. But Matt, this is another example of you keeping things from me. And it's hard for me to trust you when this stuff keeps happening."

Matt closed his eyes, "I know. I know I've been stupid. I've been making unilateral decisions and I didn't treat you like an equal partner. In the future, I promise I won't keep things from you."

Katie studied his face with a questioning look. "What are we doing, Matt? Is this a relationship? Because if it is, we're going to need to make some changes. I can't stand you doing things without telling me. It makes me feel like you don't trust me and I sure as hell am having a hard time trusting you."

"I trust you, Katie, of course I do. I was trying to protect you."

"I'm not a fragile doll."

"I know. I know you're not. You're right, I should have told you. I should know that you can handle things. I'm sorry for underestimating you."

Katie drew her eyes up into Matt's deep blue orbs and studied them. She could tell he was contrite, so maybe she could forgive him. Again, for the second time this week.

"Okay, so where does that leave us?

"I want to keep seeing you. I want to take care of you. Maybe... maybe you could move to Boston."

Anger flared in Katie's eyes, "So what, so you can be my sugar daddy and have me close by whenever you want my body?? Damn it, Matt. What the hell? I can't believe how stupid you are."

"No! I didn't mean it that way. You have to believe me!"

Katie glared back at Matt with angry tears slipping from her eyes. "I want to believe you. But you've not said anything to convince me that you want something — a real relationship, a partnership — with me. I am not the kind of person who can just sleep with someone and not get attached. That is not me. So what about you, Matt? What are you actually doing? What do you want?"

Matt paused. "I... just know I want to be with you, Katie. Isn't that enough for now?"

Katie stared into those ocean eyes for several seconds. Internally she was asking herself, *Is it? Is it enough for now?* Part of her wanted to say, *screw it all, yes, it was. It could be enough*. But another part of her thought, *Hell no. I want it all. I'm not settling. If he doesn't love me, then it's not enough. I can't love him and not have him love me back. I can't do a one-sided relationship. It's all or nothing for me.*

Matt sensed the moment Katie's attitude hardened again. Katie responded, sadly this time, "No. I'm sorry. It's not. I want a real, honest relationship with someone I love who I know loves me back. One with mutual trust. Whatever this is – was – between us, clearly, it's not that. I can't keep going with this – with a physical relationship – knowing that it's never going anywhere serious. I think it's best we just end it now."

The room was deadly silent, only the sound of their soft breathing was audible. Matt was internally screaming, NO! But he couldn't manage any words, let alone the words he thought Katie wanted to hear. He closed his eyes in defeat, and got up, ashamed of himself, and left the apartment without speaking.

21

Courage

Matt went straight to his car and started driving. He didn't know where he was going, but he knew that he had to get out and go SOMEWHERE. Katie's words bounced around in his brain like a pinball: *What do you want? What do you want?* He knew he wanted Katie. He wanted to be with her and see that smile and watch her cute expressions and see her happy. And the sex was good, so good. Shit. But what else? What comes after that?

He found himself driving through Old Orchard Beach and thinking about their date there. He observed the people, couples holding hands, feeding each other pier fries, sharing ice cream cones, and realized he was having a hard time with the "after that" part. He was so afraid of loss, of being hurt. His mom and dad were gone. He had lost his college girlfriend whom he thought he would marry. He lost Danny all those years ago. He lost everyone. Could he really do that again? Put himself out there? The thought of being with Katie for real, of letting himself fall and then losing her filled him with terror.

He got back to the apartment late, not because he was sleepy but because he didn't have anywhere else to go. He tossed and turned all night, but the answers he sought never came. Come morning, he really wanted to talk to Katie, to make things right, but realized that he didn't know what to say. *I'm a fucking coward*, he thought as he carelessly shoved clothes into a duffle bag and prepared to go back home. To Boston. He left his mom's apartment and vowed to call the charity first thing Monday morning to come get everything that was left. He started down the stairs but paused when he saw Maggie, who had stayed with Katie last night, coming up the stairs carrying coffee and a paper bag.

Matt stopped and stared at the older woman, who looked at him with a surprised expression. "Are you leaving?" she asked. Matt swallowed hard and nodded. Now Maggie looked a little pissed. "Just like that? You're not going to try again? You're not going to fight for her?"

Matt looked away and tried to speak despite the knot stuck in his throat. "I ... I don't know ... I don't know if I can give her what she needs," he finished sadly.

Maggie looked at him with fire in her eyes. "Then you don't deserve her." She pushed her way past Matt and continued up the stairs. Matt just stood there for several seconds, debating, considering, but in the end, he was too much of a coward. He continued down the stairs and out the door and back to Boston.

—•—

Matt spent the next few days immersed in work and trying desperately to not think about what a complete screwup he was. He was a tyrant at work, which was so unlike him that the staff asked Joe to intervene.

Late Tuesday afternoon, Joe knocked on Matt's office door. "What?" growled Matt. Joe opened the door and entered the office. "Matt. What the fuck?"

Matt looked up to his partner and friend, who he had known and trusted for years, the only person who could say that to him at work. He narrowed his eyes, "What?"

Joe came in and plopped down on a chair across from Matt's desk. "The staff is afraid to breathe in front of you, you've been such a terror lately. What is going on?"

"Nothing," Matt said again, looking back at his computer. Joe obviously knew about Katie but didn't know about Friday night. Matt was too ashamed and could not bring himself to relate the events to his friend.

Joe just looked at him closely without speaking for several minutes. "You went to Portland Friday, right?" Matt only nodded without looking up from his computer. Joe continued, "Something happened." It was a statement, not a question. Matt did not respond but Joe saw him stiffen.

Joe knew there was something going on, and whatever it was, it was big. Matt was clearly upset, maybe more troubled than Joe had ever seen him, though he'd never admit it. But he also knew it was not going to be easy to get Matt to talk. He considered another moment.

"Let's go grab a drink after work. You can tell me about it."

"I have too much work to catch up on." Matt said lamely.

"Bullshit. You've got to talk about it, Matt. And I want to listen." Several beats passed as Matt considered. Having a few drinks sounded good. Maybe he could even get drunk and forget his troubles for a while. *Shit. Now I'm a fucking cliche*, he thought to himself. "Fine," he acquiesced.

Joe smiled a wry smile. "Let's say six o'clock. I'll come by. Please try not to be a dick to the staff in the meantime." Matt only grunted in acknowledgement as Joe left.

—•—

A few hours later they were sitting at a bar, taking shots, and getting a little too drunk since they skipped dinner. Matt had told Joe about everything that happened that night, everything Katie said, everything he said — and didn't say. Joe listened intently, occasionally offering small commentary, until Matt finally ran out of things to say.

Joe took another shot and sat quietly for a few minutes, processing. Finally, after a long pause, he looked at Matt and said, "You are a stupid mother fucker, you know that?"

Matt was not expecting that. "What do you mean, asshole?" he said defensively.

Joe looked at him, with blurry eyes and disbelief. "Seriously? You cannot be that stupid. I went to college with you. I know you have a brain rattling around inside that pretty head."

"What?" Matt asked again. He too was a little blurry-eyed and feeling a bit dizzy from the shots, but he was pretty sure he wasn't so far gone that he missed something obvious.

Joe signaled the bartender for another round, and they were presented with two more shots shortly after. "Dude. She wants a commitment. That's all you had to say. What's the problem? You've been in love with her since day one anyway. Why not just let her know?" Joe took a shot. Matt looked a bit shocked but took his shot as well.

"I'm not sure," he mumbled.

"What? Not sure if you're in love?" Joe started laughing hysterically. Matt only glared at his cackling friend. After a minute, Joe managed to stop. He dramatically wiped the tears from his eyes and looked at his longtime friend.

"Matt, why are you fighting this? She seems amazing. She's nothing like Jessica." Matt had flinched at the mention of his ex's name but said nothing as he stared silently into the empty shot glass he was holding. He suddenly signaled to the bartender, feeling a strong need to drink more.

Once the shots came, he took one quickly as if to steel his nerves against the admission he was about to make. "Joe, I can't stand the thought of… loving her and then losing her. Everyone… everyone leaves me. Except you."

Joe looked at his friend, so obviously heartbroken and defeated, and struggled to find the words that he thought Matt needed to hear. He finally settled on this: "I think you should think about your future without her. What that would really look like and how that would feel. Then you need to think about what your future would be with her. And then, you need to decide if that possible future is worth taking a chance. Life has no guarantees, that's true. No one can make this decision for you. But honestly, I think you know in your heart what you want. Now you just have to have the courage to go get it."

Matt had no response to that.

❦

It was Thursday afternoon. Katie's shift at the bank was almost over. Today had been a good day. The lawyer had called her a few hours ago saying that, in light of recent events, Jack had withdrawn his petition for custody of Tyler.

Katie had been so intensely relieved that tears had rolled down her face without her even realizing it.

She was planning to tell Tyler when she got home, and then they'd go somewhere special to celebrate. Katie was feeling happy and hopeful that their future would be, well, if not exactly great, then at least good. She was smiling as she closed out her drawer when she heard someone enter the lobby. She turned to greet the customer but was shocked to see Matt standing there, looking intense and ridiculously handsome in black pants and a blue button-up shirt that brought out the blue in his eyes.

Katie swallowed with some effort and frantically debated how to handle this development, but her mind seemed to have short-circuited, and she couldn't manage to do or say anything at all. She just stood there, staring at that handsome face, trying desperately to not let those amazing memories float to the surface. Maggie watched with interest and protectiveness.

Matt had never been so scared in his life. His heart was thudding so loudly in his chest he was sure that Katie could hear it from across the room. But she hadn't run away yet, so that was good, right?

He tentatively stepped closer until he could see her face more clearly. She was beautiful as always, despite the yellowing bruise that still marred her face. He swallowed hard, pushing away the anger at Jack that was rising in his chest.

"Hi, um, can we talk?" he asked. Katie paused for only a second but then nodded and said, "Just let me finish up here." When she was done with work tasks and had gathered her purse, they walked together in silence out of the lobby and to the front of the building. Maggie followed and asked Katie, "Are you sure you'll be okay? I could stay with you."

"No, thanks, Maggie. I'm fine. I'll call you." Maggie nodded and went to her car, but she refused to drive away until she saw Katie was all right.

Matt saw a small city park across the street and asked if they could talk there. Katie nodded and they made their way to a bench skirting the park. There was no one nearby, so they could talk in relative privacy.

Matt sat down and turned to face toward where Katie was sitting. He nervously fiddled with his fingers. He had rehearsed this over and over and over, and he just had to say it now to Katie. He could do this. He would NOT be a coward this time. He took a deep breath and looked at Katie's expectant face and vowed not to screw this up.

"Katie. I'm so sorry. I've been so stupid. I need you to know that I was afraid, terrified really, of losing you. I lost everyone, my mom and dad, my best friend, and ... and Jessica too. And I was blind and stupid to not recognize my true feelings and what we had. Have, I hope. This is not just a fling for me. I ... I love you. And I think I have loved you from the start. And the thought of going through life without you makes me feel so sad and empty and distraught. I just can't bear it. So I want, no I NEED you to know that if you will have me, I will spend every day of my life trying to make you happy. And ... "

Matt paused to pull a small black velvet box from his pocket. Katie's breath hitched and soft tears began to leak from her eyes. Matt got down on one knee directly in front of Katie and opened the box to show a white gold ring with a large square-cut diamond in the middle. Matt looked up, into those big, beautiful puppy-dog eyes, filling now with tears, and got out the last of it.

"Katie, I know I've not proven myself to you yet, but if you give me the chance, I promise I will spend every day of my life proving to you that I love you and trust you and that I am committed to you. And when you really, truly believe me, then, if you want to, I'd love to get married and spend the rest of my life with you."

Katie burst into tears and covered her face with her hands. She cried for several seconds while Matt nervously tried to work out if this was a good cry or a bad cry. He was hoping and praying it was a good cry. *Please, God, let her say yes*, he thought over and over and over until finally she looked up at him through wet eyelashes, and he was immensely relieved that those brown eyes were shining and happy.

"Matt, that was perfect. So…yeah." Katie smiled softly, her face still wet.

Matt was almost too afraid to believe his own ears. "Yeah?" he smiled a bit and looked expectantly at this woman he loved so much.

"Yeah," Katie said again and leaned forward to kiss him, gently, slowly, with love. Matt's heart was practically jumping out of his chest with happiness and relief, and when they separated, Katie reached up to wipe a tear that had escaped from those beautiful blue eyes. "I love you too, you idiot," she whispered.

Epilogue: Dreams
Two years later

Katie was excitedly bopping around the living area of the lake house on Sebago Lake that she and Matt had purchased last summer. She was so excited for her friend Grace to arrive and to begin the festivities leading up to her wedding to Matt on Saturday. She was straightening chairs and wiping non-existent specks of dust off the furniture as she tried to distract herself from the monotony of waiting.

Katie, Matt and Tyler spent many weekends here during the summer, and it was her favorite place, so peaceful and quiet, away from the noise of Boston, where they lived most of the time. The three of them had been there for a few days already and Joe, who would be Matt's best man, had arrived late last night. Maggie and Stanley had come earlier in the week as well. They were just waiting for Grace, who would be Katie's maid of honor. Katie hadn't seen her friend and former roommate for a while, so she was eager for Grace to arrive.

Matt watched Katie from his seat in a comfy chair and smiled to himself. She was so cute and energetic, and yes, he knew she was nervous, but in a good way. Just a few weeks ago she had finished her undergraduate degree in business and was going on for a graduate degree in September. He was so proud of how hard she worked and how well she did in school, and well, just her in general. He silently thanked the universe for the millionth time for bringing her into his life and making it whole.

He glanced over at Tyler, who had been growing like a weed, almost as tall as Matt now. He seemed to have adjusted well to life in Boston and was, as far as Matt could tell, a normal 14-year-old. He was grateful that he and Katie were doing well by her "little" brother and smiled with satisfaction at the thought of their small but happy family.

When Grace's rental car finally pulled up to the lake house, Katie rushed out to greet her friend. The others followed, Matt grinning the whole time and Tyler looking a bit bored. After Grace parked, she exited the car to meet her friend. At first, all the others could see was a tangle of long, fiery red hair swooshing around as Grace hugged Katie tightly.

When the two broke their hug, Katie made introductions. "Grace, you already know Matt. And this is my little brother, Tyler." Tyler rolled his eyes at the "little" part but said hi. Then Katie continued, "These are our friends Maggie and Stanley that I've told you all about. And this is Joe Mura, Matt's business partner and best man. Everyone, meet Grace O'Leary."

When Joe went closer to shake hands, he was taken aback by the sight in front of him. Grace's red hair cascaded in gentle waves down her back and over her shoulders. She had a smattering of freckles across the bridge of her nose and on the pale skin of her cheeks. And her eyes. Joe could not believe how unique her eyes were. They were the most amazing shade of gold, like pools of honey, rich and deep.

They reached out to shake hands and when their skin touched, a shock went up Joe's arm. Startled, he looked up to Grace's deep golden eyes. She was looking at him with curiosity, and he realized he was staring and holding her hand for longer than necessary. He self-consciously dropped his hand away and looked down, chastising himself for losing his mind over a pretty face. What the hell was that?

Grace was intrigued. She was used to men being a bit taken aback by her appearance, unique as it was, but there was something about Joe that was different. She felt the intrusion of his green eyes studying her and was momentarily frozen. He was definitely handsome in a clean-cut sort of way, with his short blonde hair and those striking green eyes. But something about the way he was looking at her... Grace mentally shook herself. She was here for Katie's wedding, not to meet a guy, but damn, he was fine to look at.

Matt helped Grace with her suitcase, and they all made their way into the house. They were comfortably talking and catching up, discussing the upcoming wedding and recent life events.

Katie, snuggled in Matt's lap, was observing her friends and family gathered around the fireplace. As she took it all in, she could not believe how incredibly happy she was to be here, at this minute, in this place, with these people. She and Tyler had come so far, and there was so much further to go and so much she wanted to do. And she could do it now. She closed her eyes to savor the moment for just a little longer, and thought to herself, *my dreams came true.*

CPSIA information can be obtained
at www.ICGtesting.com
Printed in the USA
BVHW042318071121
621058BV00007B/50

9 781737 761204